BIRGITTA TROTZIG

Queen

Translated from the Swedish by Saskia Vogel

Afterword by Hanne Ørstavik

archipelago books

Published with permission by Bokförlaget Faethon.
First published in Swedish as "Drottningen" from *Levande och döda* by Bonniers

First Archipelago Books Edition, 2026

Library of Congress Cataloging-in-Publication Data available upon request.
ISBN 9781962770538
The authorized representative in the EU for product safety and compliance is eucomply OÜ, Pärnu mnt 139b-14, 11317 Tallinn, Estonia, hello@eucompliancepartner.com, +33 757690241

Archipelago Books
232 3rd Street #A111
Brooklyn, NY 11215
www.archipelagobooks.org

Distributed by Penguin Random House
www.penguinrandomhouse.com

Cover art: Color woodcut titled "Spring Night and Willow" by Nikolai Astrup, 1917-1927, 348 × 275 mm. Copyright © Musea i Sogn og Fjordane.
Photo: Thomas Widerberg, 2025.

This translation was generously supported by the Swedish Arts Council.

Archipelago Books gratefully acknowledges the generous support from the Jan Michalski Foundation, the Carl Lesnor Family Foundation, the Hawthornden Foundation, the New York City Department of Cultural Affairs, and the New York State Council on the Arts with the support of the Office of the Governor and the New York State Legislature.

Printed in Canada

Queen

To a farm in Bäck in Ljungby parish in eastern Skåne there came one day a letter announcing that a widow from America was on her way at the expense of the American government. She came across the Atlantic. Her destination was one of the villages north of the Landö lighthouse on Skåne's east coast, of the sort where the courtyard farmhouses' great barn doors face the coastal wetlands. In the summer the doors are for the most part left open and one can look right through the barn, as if it were a massive gateway, upon the pastures and the sea – the still gray sea beneath the white sky gives off a light like nothing else in this world; mild, sick; a misty white light, as mute as the blind milk of membrane around an extinguished eye; in this silent white light rest meadows so green, and the sound of steps or hoofbeats vanish without echo in the soft greensward, there reigns the silence, the birds, the scent of grass, the scent of broom, and between the people too a membrane-like silence: the white soft light upon the meadows, between the buildings, inside the buildings – words drown, the fate of the word is to drown, is it not? Children here learn that silence is golden and it is indeed so, nothing can ever be said anyway. It is the way it is. And wintertime the sea speaks, what does a person have to add to that? Winter nights through, it thunders from the darkness, the land is flat, the driving winds tend toward storm and the sea is so close, like a wild horseman the wind charges forth out in the darkness and it sounds as if the whole Baltic Sea were spilling across the meadows, rising to the barn doors, the people wake and harken, all the while inside their dreams the children hold their breath: will the gates hold? or is the sea about to wash over them with no chance of escape?

The beam of Landö lighthouse sweeps across sea, across night. Without reply.

One such night in early November 1930, during the depression, a woman alighted from a train at Ljungby Station. It was the 20:03 train, the last of the day; it was dark and had been for hours. She'd seen nothing of the parts through which she'd traveled. Neither could she see any of this landscape, whether there were forests or plains: behind the lit-up station building was nothing but impenetrable darkness, in the darkness a distant rumble could be heard, it was the mumble and roar of the Baltic but this she did not know, she'd never gone to school and knew little of how the world was constituted. She had a flat young face that looked like a child's, she could have been taken for a fourteen-year-old, a not particularly developed fourteen-year-old – in contrast to what was child-like, her unripe, mild humdrum unmoving flat little face, the sudden heft of her womanly hips made it seem as if her body from the hips down were self-contained, there a heavy being had borne and endured a life that had passed her face by; her belly was rounded as if she were a mother several times over (though she'd never carried a child to term). She wore a long cumbersome black coat that looked like a refashioned man's overcoat – it wasn't the sort of garment one should wear, it was a garment that inevitably drew all eyes to her. She looked unusual. She didn't look like people did. Her hair was black and parted down the middle, headscarf knotted good and tight below her chin: she looked like what she was, a farm girl or woman from deepest Europe. But she was coming from New York: something had happened to her there. And now she could remember but little – items, stains, fragments. As if something had burst. And she could feel no more. Only fear – but not the fear of something, just fear as something (a lump, a stone, a dead fetus) gleaned dimly beneath a stiffened, already crackling, discolored fine-grained surface. She was an empty box: playing across its plundered deep interior was an eternally flickering reflection, tall flame-shadows. Her interior had been emptied and now was full of fireshadows, shadows solely.

The train had departed. The man with the cap went inside the station, paused in the waiting room to look at a noticeboard, then unlocked a door. Through the bright window his head appeared, face sealed and strict but his lips were moving, presumably he was balancing the ticket-office register, for the train that had departed was the last of the day. The woman stood alone on the empty platform, only she had stepped off here. The rain began to pour. A little down the tracks lay the goods warehouse, which resembled a rough-hewn wooden box illuminated by a lantern high upon a telephone pole; beyond the pole and the sharply defined cone of light falling on the closed warehouse and the empty loading dock seemed to be the start of a pine forest or a grove. A muddy road slunk into the darkness towards the sound of the sea. Not one light, not one suggestion of human habitation was to be seen.

So she stands, here, looking down the road's muddy tracks into the strange darkness, the muddy village road leading into the strange land, into the strange darkness. She looks around toward the bright window on the station's ground floor. The man in the cap is standing inside, he's occupied with something. Then he goes into the waiting room, opens the outer door. He stands in the doorway for a moment, his cap still on but pushed up his forehead. He stands there. He is quite close but seems very far away. He stands there under the dripping balustrade and breathes in the rainy darkness, cap up his forehead, half his face lit up by the light inside, white and inscrutable, his eyelids seem snow-white, heavy and wrinkled: the face of one dead – so he appears to her from out in the darkness – what does a dead man look like? she never did have the chance to see him, only a charred sticky mass under the tarpaulin. Then the man in the doorway shoves his cap back in place, walks in, and locks the door behind him. The light in the waiting room is turned off, soon thereafter the inner room goes dark, the whole station building has now gone dark. Now she can hear the obscure landscape soughing and whispering around her. It smells of salt. It also smells of soil. Between the two deeply grooved tracks in the mud road lay trampled horse droppings, the scent of wet withered leaves comes streaking through the rain, upon the gusts of wind dank fresh putrefaction. A smell of fish. A smell of straw and dung. Seed and animal bodies, hot loin. It is dark. The road runs into the impenetrable.

A top-floor window lights up. She spends a while looking up at it: her stare is questioning, as if she were waiting for someone to come down after all and show her the way. But of course no one comes. She takes half a step toward the station. Then she turns around: for a moment she stares, making no move toward the darkness out there. Then she starts down the mud road, into darkness.

At the farm in Bäck one hundred years ago there was a pounding at the front gate one winter twilight. But the gate was locked, barred and bolted with the greatest care, the rectangular farmyard was now like a fortress. Twilight fell upon the snow and the farms one day, one hard winter, one lean winter: this farm like all the others was barred and bolted, impregnable.

Those who were outside, they came at dusk and pounded on the gates which stayed shut.

For in a year such as this no farm had more than what those within the farm needed for themselves.

The farms resembled fortresses, dark against the dimming sea.

From village to village roved flocks of those who had nothing, the old and unfit, and women who stumbled onward in the snow with silent gray infants in their arms, infants with gray scabby faces and white eyes. But the farmers left the bars and bolts and locks in place for no one had more than what he needed for himself. And the gates had to be barred with care for the faltering shadow-and-rag-creatures would from time to time fling themselves at them like madmen, they hammered and rattled, pounded and pulled and howled.

The blows to the gate resounded through the farm in Bäck.

In the winter twilight nearly one hundred years ago a boy named Johan Lindgren crouched beneath the kitchen window so that he could peer out, without himself being seen. He was the son on this farm. The adults sat on the settle along the inner wall, they sat unmoving, every one with their hands tightly clasped, white knuckles. At the head of the table sat the boy's father, he was a lay assessor and a great man in these parts. The fire flickered in the stove. The fire flickered upon each unmoving face. The father sat unmoving.

The boy peered cautiously out the kitchen window. It was then he saw a woman with a child. She was quite a tall woman, he'd never seen her before, she wasn't from the parish. She was tall and dark. Her face was white. Her hunger was dark. Death was dark. The snow was white. But now she was holding the child in such a curious way, arms out, the child outstretched, arms out she was holding outstretched an unmoving stiff light child's body, no telling if it was a boy or girl. She was holding it out before her as if she wanted to show it to someone, but now who would have seen it? The adults in the farmhouse weren't looking out (wise from the damage, for often pebbles rained upon the window), they sat not moving on the wide settle along the wall, a settle that could hold a good fifteen people. The woman stood in the snow, holding the body of the child before her, arms outstretched. The boy looked into the light of the fire flaming his father's face, his father's face of stone, the flames passed through his clear stone-eyes. A great heavy pale beautiful face beneath his beard: stone. The blows resounded through the farm in Bäck. The woman stood out in the snow. Above the farm and the snowlands and the sea vaulted the darkening ice-sky.

Dark is death, dark is hunger, the white white drift. Such is death's bitter empty field, death's splendid garden. She was tall and dark. She raised up the child's body before her.

The boy saw the father's face: stone, flames passed through his clear stone-eyes. The blows on the front gate died away.

Johan Lindgren rose on his tiptoes against the kitchen window. But he could no longer see the woman, only a few dark shadows in the snow at the gate, bundles together sunk into the drift. The fire passed through the clear stones of the father's eyes.

The boy who was called Johan Lindgren was born in 1850 in Bäck, Ljungby, Kristianstad County. It was an overpopulated region at that time; in difficult winters the farms had to be barred up like fortresses as defense against all the beggars who would come. He was the only son in the farthermost farm in Bäck, it was a farm that at that time had made its owner a well-to-do man, the farmer of the farm back then, that boy's father, had even been a lay assessor in his prime.

Of the villages with barn doors facing the sea, Bäck lay nearest the coast – the village was called Bäck for through it ran a brook, it ran north. And one day in early November 1930, during the depression, it happened that around dinner time the taxi cab (there was only one in the area) stopped at the farthermost farm, first out of the car was the village constable, second a small woman wearing a headscarf and a cumbersome dark coat by all indication a refashioned men's overcoat. She looked unusual. She didn't look as people did.

The farm in question was farthermost in the village – last in line; but unlike the other farms it wasn't the farmhouse but the barn that turned its long side to the village road. On the other farms the farmhouse with their long rows of windows, six or eight of them with lowered faded curtains facing the road – so that it looked as if one were walking along a row of blind buildings fast asleep (under the row of tall ash-trees, between the trunks one could see a seemingly endless, treeless plain) all the way until one arrived at the last farm: a sealed smooth clay-daubed barn wall, a single barred black wooden hatch up on the wall made it look even more shut and sealed. From the road the farmhouse couldn't be seen, it was lateral to the barn and was only visible from within the farm – then it could be seen between barn and sheds, due south and with a sheltered and sunny front garden, unusually lush and blooming in the summer. The daughter, Judit (in these parts she was called Queen, a singular and distant and unyielding person not the sort to take advice from others) had a love of lilies, she had two beds full of the large white kind – what a vision it was when they were in bloom! The short path up to the large steps (the entrance that was never used more than once or twice in a human lifetime) was lined with shells that also resembled large white lilies, but petrified.

The frontside garden, which faced south, was Judit's pride, however overburdened with work she was she never neglected it. But at the house's other side, the north side, was more of a wilderness, a wilded meadow but with gray-leaved choke pears and bergamots (though they no longer bore ample fruit) sloping toward the brook that gave the village its name. By the brook was also an alder grove – but apart from it was not one tree, from the chamber windows to the east and north was a wide view of the sea and up the coast and thereafter not one tree interrupted the horizon.

This had once been a large and prosperous farm. Going by the buildings alone it was still the largest in the village – but it was apparent that prosperity had long since moved on, the buildings were in disrepair. The barn did seem fairly well-maintained, but the state of the sheds suggested that they'd long been too many and too large for what the farm yielded. On one, the side of the roof facing the sea had collapsed – but even the other roofs were sagging, thatching thick with layers of brown moss and full of holes that revealed glimpses of bared laths. And everything was like this, warped, wrecked, strung together, serviceably repaired but in fact not serviceable: it was apparent in all things that those to whom the farm belonged in fact couldn't handle it, apparent overall were efforts wrecked and stranded, it was as if they'd left scars behind: works begun, begun and abandoned attempts at repair.

The farm was now owned and run by a pair of siblings, Judit and Albert Lindgren, both in their fifties – they were born only a year apart. Their father Johan Lindgren in Bäck, he was by now long dead; and even longer dead now was his father, the one who'd been the lay assessor and well-to-do. There'd been a third, a much younger brother who'd gone to America and from whom nothing had been heard for a good many years. He was called Viktor, Viktor Gustaf Lindgren (Gustaf after the paternal grandfather, the lay assessor, a symptom of the father's bad conscience about truly not being able to stand the sight of the newborn, so at least he'd be given a proper name – Viktor Gustaf); he'd been named as the father of several children in the area and so had reason not to leave too precise an address – albeit the siblings in silence did pay all that was demanded of such. Without comment – not a word of censure against the runaway brother ever passed their lips. Neither the sister's, nor the brother's; he followed her and obeyed her in all. But the chairman of the child welfare board knew that even so these pains should be kept as succinct as possible: nothing superfluous during such visits – no mention of the weather, nor anything else – no accepting the offer of coffee, above all no jocularity. For pained it was. It was written on Judit's face as she opened the kitchen door and saw what manner of visitor had come; it was written on the bent tired hunch of her back as she trudged across the floor to unlock the chiffonier where she kept a cache of money. She was always the one to handle these arrangements like she was the one who always had hold of the reins; there was something hazy about Albert that couldn't quite be grasped, it would have felt senseless to turn to him for a matter of such import. Judit, she was called Queen for she had a loftiness about her; stately and stern but present: she had good sense, she knew to differentiate between bad and good, between what was true and the fluid imaginary – well, no wonder she was brusque, folks said, toiling alone on that farm with only Albert for help. Albert such as Albert now was: without question a great reader of the Bible, but there was something about his thoroughly common intelligence that did not feel reassuring, not dishonest exactly (for one who never says a word can hardly be said to be lying), but he had a shifting sort of timid gaze, far too sensitive.

But Judit was Judit. Bad. Good. Said was said, done was done.

But Judit never complained about Albert, she didn't speak of him at all.

Of the other one, during his time at home – of him she had spoken. Far and wide even. Well, at first. Then with greater insecurity: yes yes

I suppose we'll have to see after his military service. Later badly – without bounds. As though there were a spring of hatred inside her, all the words in the world were insufficient, there were so few words in this rough land's laconic language, those were in fact silent, so the spring of hatred simply welled and welled.

Then he set off and stayed away.

And Judit fell silent, she never said another word about her favorite brother who she'd borne in her arms, fed and raised. Nor about Albert – that it was Albert and not the other one who stayed with her, of this she did not speak. Besides, when it came down to it, he was of help to her; when he wasn't having one of his headache days he worked according to his ability; he was strong and diligent if slow; he did what he could.

But Judit managed to do twice of what she was capable of. In these parts, they called her Queen. And she was queen of rags, of sagging moldering roofs, of nothing. And with each passing day the bank claimed yet another piece of her domain.

And the Queen had wanted something different. Of something completely different had she dreamed, this Queen.

The lighthouse beam swept through the dark. Over sea, through night.

Now there walked on the farm a sister and a brother. There had once been a father and a mother.

To them had first been born a daughter, it was clear she could shoulder and endure, that she was to be relied upon: Judit.

Barely a year later a boy child came into the world, he was christened Albert, he was big and strong, but the paternal grandfather who was still alive and ruling immediately took measure of the boy's worth – from the very start the boy was as if set to one side, among those who weren't to be counted on. But the boy's father (who during the lay assessor's long lifetime never was allowed much of a say on the farm, he mostly went around there like a farmhand made to obey, this lasted too long, this removed from him the very taste and lust for life) felt great tenderness for this child who they said wasn't good for much, who was sluggish, dull and weak-minded, a bit dishonest, quick to tears – he took the boy with him into the field, collected rocks and mussel shells for him to play with as he sat at the edge of the field, often he let horse and plow stand and came to sit next to the little one, sometimes he took him in his arms and they'd sit like this a long while, in stillness. Albert also turned to his father when he was small. This was when he was very small. Then at length the grandfather died and the father became the farm's lone farmer; with this his perception of the boy shifted, at once he understood that there wasn't much to Albert, his grandfather had been correct. So he let him be. But he'd often take his hand if they were to go off somewhere, he did so carefully as if afraid of rousing someone from a fragile slumber.

The girl Judit however attended to her brother, they were never on bad terms. But often time was short, she wasn't supposed to be playing after all, she was supposed to help her mother, she toiled like an adult with dishes and laundry while her brother lay on the kitchen floor playing with wooden logs – she was saddled with much more than her strength could bear (it was also a long way to school against the icy wind in winter) and for a long time she stalled in her growth, gray and stooped. But she mustered the strength. For she knew that her father and her mother relied on her, she felt as if everything depended on her. She never had much time to be a child, but neither did she value such things: her soul had been old and mature from the start. And something in her body responded to the burden she was handed, something in her was unbreakable – one day the girl straightened up (under the yoke and water buckets) and grew, she grew to be stately and strong and in her way beautiful.

A few years after Albert, their mother miscarried her unborn child, it died inside her and arrived dead in the world, a five-month-old girl-fetus. And only after a number of years, eight years after Albert, did she birth another – a boy who would remain the youngest. Very ill after the birth, she lay white and breathless inside the chamber. She was battling for her life, the village doctor came and said it was time for her to visit the infirmary. But the infirmary was far, she couldn't be taken there in this state. And then she seemed to improve somewhat. And then she never did get on her way.

But while their mother lay inside gasping for her life in the chamber while they waited for their father to return with the doctor, the woman who was there to help with the newborn came into the kitchen where the two children were sitting petrified on the sofa (the boy weeping slowly and crying mostly because the atmosphere was so grisly: so baffling) and she laid the newborn in the nine-year-old's arms: Take him, girl – soon he'll have no mother but you! It was a sort of initiation. The boy, who was later christened Viktor Gustaf, lay this way in her arms, a warm weight, breathing and alive. He was warm and curious to touch, he breathed with small light powerful breaths, his eyes were squeezed shut as though in the few hours he'd been alive he had already managed to be horror-struck by something obscure and grim – his eyes and the small rough red face were squeezed tight as if he were trying in vain to shield himself from a harsh light or an attack. The girl held him in her unpracticed arms, the holding became heavy and unwieldy, tiring. He slept with balled-up fists and that little strong body felt hard and tense, it was as if he couldn't fit into her embrace – as if even in his sleep, a newborn's light warm animal-sleep, he was resisting: at odds, on guard. She felt her arms begin to tremble and lose their strength. But she did not let go, her entire body drew itself around him, in a hard stiff grip – but then it occurred to her to begin to rock him very slowly back and forth to ease the hardness. Suddenly his quick breaths halted, it was as if he'd stopped breathing and the girl's heart sank. Then she saw that he'd awakened and was looking up at her face. His eyes were shining with a curious strong pale-blue color from the dark red folds of skin, his wrinkled eyelids fine as silk. Could he see her? Or what was he seeing? The shining slits of his eyes held little of a gaze: it was more like a sharpness springing forth, a streak of light or gleaming water.

With this the little one was hers. And she was his. From here on and hereafter this was her task, felt the girl as she sat, straight-backed, on the settle in this unusually tiring position. Albert beside her, a heavy tear-streaked eight-year-old in too-tight clothing outgrown in every way (trousers straining, shirt gaping across his chest, everything chafing and worrying), drew a deep sigh, impossible to judge by the sound whether this was the final snuffle of his weeping or the beginning of a fresh long quaking floe of sobs. To make sure the girl turned her head and looked him over; thereupon she said quite sharply:

"Oh Albert, enough now, can't you see you're waking him!"

The brother caught mid-sob. It was as if he'd frozen. For this marked a turn.

He wanted to turn to her, he did so often, blind and soft like a calf to the cow.

And now it wasn't possible. It wasn't possible.

Judit didn't meet his gaze. She looked down at the infant in her arms. Her eyelids were lowered. Unwavering lay the shadow of long dense eyelashes over the girl's wan cheek.

(Amid what was as yet ungrown, sometimes a look. A sudden shining. Then gone. A girl's strong chapped red hands had she. Along with bouts of fickleness and cruelty, out of the blue an utterly different being might come charging. And then – gone again! Once more strict and stern and not to be toyed with. Such glimpses were few and far between. But one knew it was there. Deep inside, shining.)

She was all he had. She'd always been there. She was his. And this is how it was to be, this was how it had to be. She helped. For she was not afraid. With him it was as if the very gesture of doing things or taking things on or telling someone something was uncertain, half-inhibited, in some way weakened and impotent from the start. But Judit was not afraid. She took him by the hand. Then it worked. Then it was as it should be.

Otherwise there was much, a near majority, nearly all the time, that was not as it should be. From the start everything was difficult, too heavy. He got so tired. Then his head ached. (And as if in some inscrutable way they perceived him as soft, somehow rotten inside, weak, the girls at school chased him, inexhaustibly, monotonously, it was the great joy of recess, they ran after him and pinched him and shrieked: lard-butt! lard-butt! they shrieked until he burst into tears, this was also about how easily he could be made to cry). He got so tired. He bore no ill will. He was not ill-disposed toward anyone. But he didn't have the strength.

One day he played truant. He walked with Judit to school, somewhere mid-route he simply vanished: not until late in the afternoon was he found, having crawled into the darkest corner of the attic behind the flour bins, stiff with fear of the rats, but in his solitude he'd discovered something, not for his life could he have put words to it, but it was stronger than the fear of the rats. Floury white and with cobwebs in his hair he was hauled out and beaten. But he'd discovered something. It was stronger. Solitude tugged at him and enticed and whispered, he came to be of the kind who was forever seeking solitude; to which followed this was not his last time playing truant however afraid he was of a beating; suddenly he belonged to the side of truants and shirkers. It simply was, so it went. And he often had headaches.

Body stiff he looked at the newborn Judit was holding, its little face, the pale slits of its eyes, something indistinctly frightening. Something was menacing, something was hostile. Inside the chamber their mother called out in her fever delirium. Both siblings startled, they looked at each other but Judit's eyes immediately fell upon the baby. The neighbor woman started crying in there: O God, o God – The child began to scream. Albert kept trying to catch Judit's eye.

But Judit didn't give him a single glance, she was rocking that screaming boy, lips moving gently.

The boy Viktor had been placed in her arms. And with that he was hers. And she was his.

And even after the mother was back on her feet (which took a while) it was so that Judit was more a mother to him than she – to the extent that it was possible Judit was the one to mind him, often she had to stay home from school, their mother only had the energy for the essentials. Milking, meals, laundry – this was already too much for her. But it was also that the mother in her indeterminate way seemed to feel an aversion toward the little one – a flinch at least (as when meeting a snake), in any case it was something she always had to overcome, swallow down, before she touched him. Perhaps her body simply couldn't help but associate the infant with fever, unbearable nausea, the fear of death. Often it was not noticeable, not clear. A blink of the eye – then it was over. As if nothing had been. But the blink of the eye *had* been. And in that blink of the eye the infant's gaze had time to take fright and find refuge in another face, in one that did not wish to cast him out. And Judit became the one to give him the bottle and change him before she left for school. Solemnly the girl sat there with the child. Far away in the dark winter morning a burning streak could be seen above the tranquil sea, it spread gradually at first, the skies began to burn, the mother blew out the kerosene lamp, their faces now caught by the sunrise-glow, like the faces of the drowning they floated up out of the kitchen's dark and shadow. Burned. Judit held the large infant in her little lap and fed him milk and sugar water and bread dissolved in water. Like Albert this one was large and heavy and had a hearty appetite. But Albert had been very calm as an infant, almost always sleeping. This one was uneasy and demanding in a different, more difficult and greedier way. In a very short time he learned that he should direct his demands to Judit, the mother didn't respond, with her all was mute. But at the slightest whimper Judit appeared, wide-awake in the middle of the night. Sometimes he woke her several times a night – first so she'd bring him close to her, next when he was lying with her on her mattress on the floor (close beside her on the other side Albert was sleeping with open mouth, but he never woke up) so she would rock him there in the warmth under the blanket and hum almost inaudibly in his ear. Thus passed the nights, one by one. And Judit was quite gray and pale in those years, leached out and with deep under-eye rings, and over the course of the day it happened that the classroom, the teacher, the children, the tiled stove spun before her eyes, everything swung one or two rounds before finding its place in reality again. But she always knew her lessons, she was foremost among her peers for it was her wish to be foremost, it was in school that she began to be called Queen – as well as for her stubborn arrogance, once she'd trained her will on something let it be as it may, she took nothing back. And there at nighttime she found her nourishment, it tempered her such that she believed she could handle anything: she vaulted her arms around her little brother and lay there with the warm often soaking-wet child pressed to her, his hot gentle breath against her neck, the boy smelled of urine, sour milk, dirty diapers, but this was simply his smell – so she lay there in the darkness and felt his breathing, his aliveness. In some way the world here in the darkness was completed, realized, it could not hold more, it could not become more – complete: filled to the brim! With a timid gesture she moved (they were children not particularly inclined toward caresses) her lips grazed the infant's hard bowed forehead. Nothing could be more whole!

The girl lay in darkness and sensed that there was no way out, out into the world for her. The crown was here, where she already was. The core was here, dense, hot, alive. There was nothing to look forward to. All that was left for her was to plummet, fall back – part ways and die. Part, subside, and then die. White as her mother on that night.

Through the darkness swept the beam. Capturing – releasing: capturing – releasing. So deep the darkness when the light released its grip, like falling down through a well, darkness, no end; again the sleepers were struck by the light as if by a knife; again darkness, all the while they were on their way into darkness downward and downward, whirling, falling. Without pause the lighthouse beam swept across ever-new light-unstruck never-seen waves.

So it was henceforth (it could be counted from the moment Victor entered into existence) as if the mother hadn't quite been present. Even though she was there; even though she did do what she could; even though she was constantly busy at the stove, with the laundry, in the dairy. She was dark-haired like Judit. But all could be surmised from that slender hesitant red hand, she wiped her forehead with the back of her hand as if she were trying to wipe away something indelible – a darkness that suddenly arrived and shrouded what was in front of her, the kitchen or the dairy walls. A piece of the separator machine shimmering metallic in the billowing dark. Or the pot handle. Like one drowning she reached for the piece she could see – a piece that seemed about to recede into the dark, the dark rose like water or fog, it billowed like the sea on a twilit autumn night. Great empty waves. She fumbled her hand across her forehead – managed to knock over a pot, felt boiling water splatter her ankles. Sank down on a chair. Darkness enclosed her fully now. The children looked upon her white face, her pale eyes. Where could she be?

Johan Lindgren, the father, was a large heavy silent man with a gentle way about him. He sat at the table in his blue-striped work shirt. He got up. He turned his gentle gaze to her, a gaze that had always been ponderous but by degrees had acquired something new, a glimmer of pained vacillation. He touched her, tried to wake her. But she did not feel his touch – his above all, so it seemed to him. He stood heavy and silent, arms slack beside her, as such he resembled a large tamed animal. No rebellion. But the pained wet-glimmer in his eyes: what have I done? Lord my God, what have I begotten? When have I betrayed – thus?

As if this hulking person were about to break into sobs. But everything was so difficult there was no point even in this – so difficult, more difficult than anything he could have imagined. Not even the sobs simmering deep inside his chest had it in them to make their way out, this is too difficult, there's no point in this, he might as well laugh instead: nothing has a point, laugh or cry all the same, the silence of life is nonetheless comprehensive, consummate. More unrelenting, more consummate it cannot be. The children look from mother to father, father to mother. All is silent. So it is.

Well, she was indeed there, they took her by the arm, gave her a tug – but she shook it off, it was as if she allowed them to slip from her. Now her eyes regained their vision: of the external. But still she was not there, she never was – she no longer had the strength to make her way back to them, she was far away and didn't have the strength to make her way back. Out in that fog something had torn her up, damaged her, this was for life. Now he had a small face, a small body – red, alive, a harmless infant. But to her someone else resided in that little body, something fully developed full of destruction. Her weak pale eyes looked lost upon the child in Judit's lap.

She'd returned superficially, as said. Albeit she could no longer quite muster the energy for life, the passage of her life would be long, and superficially she did not sit idle. But she never had the energy to make her way back to them. She'd been cracked and stayed so. Slowly life trickled out of her – a rivulet soaked up by parched earth, as if it never had existed – not a drop thereof could those powerless hands bring to that thirsting mouth. Pneumonia claimed her in the winter of 1913 as easily as one carries a child across a creek. But by then Johan Lindgren, the husband who nonetheless had come across as the stronger of the pair, had already lain in the cemetery for two years.

The girl Judit had been very attached to her father. For he had relied on her. The more empty, sparse, and silent it became around the mother – to be sure she continued to speak but her milling words were light and dead, like dead seeds – the more he would turn to his daughter. It was nothing that could be expressed in words. But a trust that was never made explicit, it was too much, it lay too deep inside, filled every moment of her childhood with its warmth.

And she carried her little brother. Carried him, minded him, sang for him, rocked him when he was sleepy; had an untiring patience with his hardships, whims, tantrums. All this in trust, without a grumble – the thought would never have occurred to her. For her father did trust her. So all was as it should be. However it was.

Nevertheless there was that occasion when the father was herding the sheep home from the coastal wetland – one autumn night turning black, turning blue. The children were with him. The sea gone dark. But the wetland shone greenish gray through twilight as if the earth had its own glow, from within. Sticks, blades were articulated with the utmost clarity in this earth-light. The children kept close to the father in the very center of the flock, the sea lay so dark and black, they walked so close to him that they felt the heat of his legs and loins, the heat of him an intimate shield, they walked hot and hidden within his heat. Far across the heath the sun was setting, face and hands shone red in the sunlight. The stone walls stretched far up the heath, far into the sunset. They took their father's hands, one had the left to himself, this was Albert – Judit and the little one who was now of course like a part of her gathered at the right, still after decades (so many decades now! right across the vaulting ravaging sea of time, with each passing year ever more clear how frighteningly quick and strong the currents suck outward! outward!) she remembered how that hand felt, the heat of its rough scarred fingers, the cracked uneven tips of his nails. Then the little one began to whine, he couldn't keep up the pace, he stopped to cry. The sheep ran onward around them, tripping, shoving, bleating. The father said: Judit, go on then, go to him, I can't bear that infernal noise!

The girl stopped to comfort the little one, she thought her father would also stop – but he kept going with Albert at his hand, the sheep kept going around her and past her, now her father was a good ways away, it was as if he hadn't noticed she was there, it was as if her obedience were a given, it was as if he hadn't seen her, it was as if he'd never seen her. The flock's steps and bleating grew distant. Also growing distant was the figure of the father and the boy he was holding by the hand. At once she saw that her father and Albert were very alike, once Albert was grown he'd seem the spit and image (perhaps in some way an image in a damaged mirror, shifting, slightly flawed at edge and line) of his father. And they appeared ever farther away. Now they were already halfway up to the farm, close to the pine grove with the well. The little one clung to her screaming, he wanted to be carried. Then she called out to her father. Call out she did. But it rang hollow in the evening as if nothing had been, father and brother continued into the clear red evening, the flock of sheep between the walls surrounding them. So after calling out she stood there with her mouth ajar.

Father and brother were far away. Unreachable they walked in the red shimmering light. They were alike. A rank, salty autumnal smell came from the sea. And a gust of mull and earth from up by the harvested fields, a damp smell of death through the heather, through the autumn twilight.

And in this moment the world was cleft. From top to bottom. Through the cleft something desolate seeped in. The little one suddenly stopped his crying and looked up at his sister. With his shimmering wet hot gaze – curiously unlike others. And she sat on the ground and brought him close to her and pressed her cheek to his little chest and began to weep.

The girl Judit, the twelve-year-old already known as Queen, had a long face that was wider at the cheeks and jaw than at the forehead. Her mouth with its full lips was beautiful. Her eyes lay as if in shadow, they seemed dark but when the light fell through the clear stones of her eyes they lit up with brilliant transparency. She wore her hair in long dark braids, otherwise the whole of her was gray, there was something colorless and arduous about her body which still mostly resembled that of a strong-limbed boy. And she sat there on the ground with the boy in her arms, her body in clenched strident sobs. But after a while she was no longer crying. Her face was at once entirely unmoving, entirely shut.

But deep within that which is locked up the weeping continues. The gray features harden, the gaze becomes clear, dark, tearless. Deep down the weeping continues. Stifled it bores itself ever deeper downward, inward, vanishing undermost in the deadest layer of earth underneath hidden crumblings, through stone chips down in the desiccated rock-hard packed stratum of the ground. There the weeping could no longer be heard, it had vanished from sight and sound, far down in the invisible, in dead earth it whimpered and sobbed.

Viktor grew: childhood is an endless span of time, not as seen from the outside but for the one within it it's a clear depth, extending under time, downward like a well, through the water shimmers darkness in motion and light. Viktor grew and grew out of his tunic and foul-smelling diapers – which they had to let him walk around in well past his third birthday, there was no other way despite all the beatings he received. In spite of his gentleness the father could not stand this, not the smell (which lingered) and not the fact of the matter itself. He took it upon himself to discern a sign of God's wrath in the impurity of his youngest – if it was not perhaps so that the boy as a whole, troublesome, obstinate, and quick to scream as he was, became one such a sign to his father: whatever the case, for one or another reason he had something against his youngest, something as insuperable as nausea. This was at a time when he was beginning in earnest to understand that his patrimony was falling through his hands, the farm seemed to be evading his grip, ends simply couldn't be made to meet, he had also spent far too much on horse-rearing (he loved animals and most of all his horses as if these beings were human, more than he'd ever had the energy to love human beings) and now he was forced to abstain from them, he could find no buyers for the yearlings anymore; but he had a hard time with the regular farm work, he seemed to have no feeling for it and the days went by, the work amassed and overwhelmed him, much had to be skipped over, much was neglected entirely, it was hard to find proper help, all the young men were going off to the States; it felt as if life itself were drifting apart for him, heavy and formless; and from his spouse there issued no life, no answer, only a type of paralysis, it grew ever heavier; everything amassed all at once, it was too much all at once. And he beat the boy to cure his impurity. And a despair, not of the kind that could find its way up to the words and secure liberation, weighted the blows. After all he was a good and patient man, if melancholic: he did not mean for the blows to be heavy. But heavy they were. At such moments Judit stared in white fear at the father: at this unrecognizable face that also belonged to him. There was no beauty in it, what made itself known when his strong, gentle face was torn off like a skin. What appeared was unrecognizable. It was not beautiful.

Then Judit noticed how afterwards the little one still red and quaking with tears would go out to punish something he could control – he tore a leaf to pieces, he mashed a worm with a rock: there! and there! take that! Judit came rushing after him to offer comfort. But the boy wanted nothing to do with her. His blows rained down: take that! take that! And he screamed at her as if she were not her at all but merely a part of all the lifeless heaviness closing in around him, an evil wall one must pound one's way through – blow after blow after blow – so as not to be stifled. Where one had to sink one's teeth in so as not to be stripped and humiliated. She squatted beside him, scratch marks on her face burning and she tried to speak to him and get him into her arms; but he resisted and turned his head away. He did not want to be comforted. And she sensed how he was closing himself off.

And she sensed how she was being left alone. As young as he was he had made himself unreachable, slick and smooth like a sea-glazed stone, no longer to be grasped. Gray sky, black nettles, chicken scratch, the cat upon the rat, down the meadows the gray expanse of sea – what did she have to do with this whole world? Alone were they, each and every one unto themself, like cast stones scattered in the empty water-dawn.

Still the father was a good person – as close as one comes to good. Perhaps. But what was in his hands, in his body was stronger. Thus rained the blows. He could not control them.

A large broad-shouldered meek man, there was something gravely violent yet absent about him. He had a large soft grizzled brown beard, large hands, there was something stifled about those hands, restrained, they opened and closed themselves often. Often as if in a cramp: opening and closing themselves. The hands of a man of violence, a fortune teller would have said. And there was violence in him. Something putrefied in darkness, that's how it was, the darkness inside him that was the darkness in such places one dares not enter after dusk – the darkness between the wind-moaning pines in the grove around which the road curved (the grove with the well) or the darkness under the bent pine where the search party once cut down the priest in Ljungby, he'd hanged himself (but that was two-hundred long years ago) – such darkness was inside him.

He pondered God's wrath. And the darkness inside himself and what inside him was insurmountable. It was a white day when he saw this in himself, he saw with the utmost clarity how it was woven together, a gray-white snow-powdered late-autumn day – he walked onto the heath, he had an errand over in Torp at the edge of the forest and he had made it up to where the road curves over the crest, he turned around and saw the whole wide heath gray-white-shimmering with snow gently sloping all the way down to the sea, it was over five kilometers down to that black-green unmoving surface, the air was gray and colorless and easy to breathe, it carried a faint fresh whiff of snow. The road curved over the crest. To the left was a pile of rocks, to the right was a spring. Around the spring a thicket of low alders, hazel – leaves fallen on the frost-gray ground like a blanket of gold coins. The spring was clear and dark. The junipers scented the still gray frosty air with dense bunches of blue berries frozen black. He looked out over the whiteness, saw the pile of rocks and the spring, the black sea far beyond and at once he saw deep inside himself, deep down in himself there took shape connected images and figures like an obscure but clear map, he could see how everything was connected. And he threw himself to the ground: child of God.

He did not much love people, they were too heavy, something about them was insurmountable to him. He loved the animals, especially horses, their warm silence as they breathed and gave a little snort.

And their stillness like foggy mornings over the coastal wetlands when the young horses drew closer with soft hoofbeats in the grass and the silence in the haze out over the water when he took up his net and the sound of water against the boat and his own heart's heavy already aged beating was all that could be heard of the world. And then like a voice within the silence, like a bird's joyful cry or a clear strident child-voice singing without age, above the ages. One long since dead. Or one not yet born to this world, a single strident clear voice out of the silence, out of the bliss beyond the ages. But people were something heavily curious, heaviest and most curious was this thing about Viktor, the youngest.

He pondered the soul of God. And his own darkness. In this he lived, saw and observed. But the business of the world slipped through his fingers, he didn't have the stamina to gather his thoughts to further his fortunes, he preferred to sell off a parcel here, a parcel there. It saved him for the moment. But soon they were without again, that which was divided and sold off of course did not return. And it seemed dates of payments due came ever more frequently. And of course he couldn't continue endlessly selling things off, so he had to go into debt instead: so he was on a treadmill, a squirrel on a wheel. Night-moments came – close to the early summer when the white unmoving light of night flowed in through the window like the very breath of sleeplessness, he writhed in his bed, rose, he stood by the bucket in the kitchen and drank from the scoop, the night-haze hung white and he understood that his lifetime would not be sufficient to get himself out of all the trouble he so quickly, without in fact realizing how, had happened into. He sat where he sat, snared. It was many long years now since the farm was a lay assessor's farm. Long since he who owned and ran the farthermost farm in Bäck was considered an important man. It was going downhill slowly but surely, the simple truth was that he'd already managed to get quite far along on this slope. And with lingering gazes and from under their bangs, the children learned to interpret the expressions on people's faces – was it contempt? – before they even dared speak when spoken to.

The roofs began to fall into disrepair, far too many stalls stood empty. In the middle of the farm lay a pile of ailing wrecked equipment that no one carted away. But in the evenings after supper, he took the Scriptures from the shelf in the cabinet above the kitchen table. He read half-aloud to himself and following the words with his index finger like schoolchildren did:

"And-the-world-passeth-away-and-the-lust-thereof-but-he-that-doeth-the-will-of-God-abideth-for-ever – " he read. Dark, open, wondering at this was his gaze. Judit had his eyes, the darkness about them, the shine from within: they were their paternal grandfather's eyes, really. Who doeth the will of God? He read again and again. And the darkness, the insurmountable?

He made a cross of gray already wind-gnawn boards and raised it against the stone wall in the farthest of the arable fields that lay before the pastures that bordered the sea. And he explained himself to no one. He said nothing. His gaze was dark and open. In moments, in glimpses, he seemed like another person to them: one they'd never seen before. But this thing about Viktor he could not control, he could not come to terms with it, it was insurmountable: he'd stopped beating him: there was a seeking distant something when he looked at him, when he – seldom – spoke to him, a pain arrived in his features as if he were straining to call out through an emptiness that devoured all sound. But no shout could penetrate the dull empty silence, it was as if they'd never exchanged a word, father and youngest son, nothing was ever received as intended. And life marched on, in the muteness, in the emptiness. Sometimes it appeared as though the boy's shining bright gaze was unseeing, blind.

Johan Lindgren in Bäck, his gates now stood open for whoever wished to pass through them, whoever so desired was provided a place at the table however lean it was for him and his family. And there was never a shortage of guests, as difficult as it was to get hold of a decent farmhand equally it was teeming with all manner of roving folks, the sugar beet campaigns attracted a great many (sometimes Poles and Germans) who'd end up staying the winter in the area sustaining themselves however they could, Swedes and others fit for work went to the States but this place was full of vagabonds, casual laborers, ordinary beggar men and beggar women, not to mention the parish's every elder, widows and biddies who supported themselves by helping out with odd jobs for the day in exchange for food and something to take home in their basket; someone was always at their table, devouring the food as if it were the last meal of their life.

One stank. One hadn't had it in him to keep his head above water, couldn't handle the endless battle to stay alive like others did, to stay fed, dressed, washed. One couldn't manage to remove himself from the sinking morass of the poor, the whirl and suction of dissolution beneath his feet. Right beneath.

Roofs fell into disrepair, stalls stood empty, and no other animals were put in them, it wasn't worth it, whichever way he turned it only seemed to end in loss and greater debt. It sucked and whirled and ate away at the narrow strip of solid ground on which they stood. A brittle patch. And the entirety of the sea lapped and ate away at it. They stood there in the middle of the sea and the ground beneath their feet was on its way out. And the children in the area who were largely aware of this, shouted after Judit across the whole schoolyard: Queen! Queen! That stuck-up nut!

In the face of the poor, we find God, said the father to the children. But Judit did not see it this way.

Someone was always at their table. The girl Judit would observe him or her, the shadowrag with the human face. She observed the shadow creature attentively. She felt her will flex like a muscle: this would not be their fate. Not hers. Not that of her brothers – even if she died trying. They would not be sucked down. She pressed the little one she was feeding to her and turned his head away so that he would not see the vagabond sitting there with quaking hands, quaking mouth.

The repugnant quivering mouth devouring the food like an animal, starved dog or cat.

It's not their fault, thought the girl. It's not their fault. But they shouldn't be allowed to exist. She observed the vagabond eating. She observed her father who with unpracticed hands served those eating. She observed them both with her adult gaze, not without compassion. But her shut-fast tightly pressed lips said: Not me. And not mine. There is a choice in this world. I know what I'm choosing. I take this upon myself. I know what I'm doing.

No, she wanted nothing to do with him. Nor with Albert – if she wanted nothing to do with the sun, neither did she want anything to do with the shadow of the sun. That's how it felt. It was a hard and empty wasteland. But I am correct, said her life to her. His life is wrong, said her life. Each and every one must stand on their own. I intend to stand on my own. I know what I'm doing. I'll take this upon myself.

She saw that the potatoes froze because they were poorly and sloppily covered. For such things he did not have the energy. He fancies himself above it, thought the girl. And she could feel herself hardening.

But it was difficult. So difficult. He sat by the kitchen table in the evening, finger following along the Scripture's words, lamp shining overhead, outside stood the night, out in the night roared the sea. The girl looked at him. And an almost unbearable tenderness rose up, it was as if she were being torn to pieces – she released a moan, a half-stifled sob. Blood-red face, she pressed her lips together and looked in another direction, her face grew dark strict and hard. Her father looked up at her, for a moment the reading stopped. But the girl's face was as old and dark as stone. Her father then lowered his gaze and his lips resumed their motion. His mighty head, his white deeply furrowed face within the beard. Lips slowly moving. The blue neckband.

(There was also this matter of being called Queen. More than a pet name. Also a secret she kept – caressed like a gemstone, caressed into heat while remaining achingly cold as stone is always stone, precious, shining clear: stone, despairing stone.)

It was difficult. For in that time – that Eastertide, that Whitsuntide – she was being prepared for confirmation. And on Whitsunday she was confirmed along with all the others who were turning fifteen that year, it was an early summer day of the kind she would remember her whole life through as *summer* – the taste, the smell: young brittle summer – and the balmy wind blew across white-blooming meadows, the brook flowed in a dizzy froth between rockfoil and sweet woodruff, the sun shone on the church walls, on the graves shone white narcissus and beyond the cemetery wall the fragrant meadows shimmered. In her black dress she thus was confirmed and ate the bread of God.

But as if this alien bread had touched something that couldn't endure being touched, someone in her (the hidden unknown Judit) collapsed quaking and at night she dreamed and the dream was filled to the brim with a gruesome terror that was as palpable as hot wet skin:

She saw many a thing: take of it and eat! Eat! But she also saw a platter (of thick white porcelain like a wash basin in shape but smaller), it floated upon the sea which was gleaming and thick as oil – how curious that the platter could float so easily, this was the platter under the Baptist's head, however the sea seemed as heavy as a mass of molten oil-thick seething lead. It floated like an eye. It moved upon the infinite.

It floated on the waves. Bearing blood froth.

Red froth washed across pale dry lips. She waited. Her limbs waited, pale, parted, dead – submerged in a heavy sweetness as in a deathly slumber. But no face was born from this frothing, it merely gaped bloody, dead.

And she awakened in a pouring sweat, her mouth wide-open, screams seemed to be clanging back at her from her chamber walls, but of course no one else in the house had awakened.

The years went by. It was the turn of the century, in the farms nothing much changed, folks went to the States, some disappeared there, others returned, others yet became rich and sent money home, not many of those, nor was it a question of large sums: the area too hardly changed, it was a poor area, money disappeared as if into something bottomless and still nothing changed. Across the sandy plains, the pastures, on the heaths was heard the ceaseless voice of the Baltic, it surged, it sank, it was always the same, times passed and through it all the waves washed up, the waves washed down the limestone rock face. And the sky was the same, the wide vault of the heavens over the low grounds where horses and sheep grazed the short rough grass. The white-tailed eagle circled high above the shoreline dark and alone, the waves pounded, the waves tore at the narrow black-tarred flat-bottomed rowboat's mooring around the rocks. The peewits called out and called across the beach meadows, they called out sorrow across the meadows, out across the endless gray waves.

The children in the farthermost farm in Bäck grew up – the two oldest so like their parents one might think the clock had been turned back, that the young pair of humans from twenty years ago now walked here again; and those who were old now were the old ones from then; all alike, all coming around again; the father albeit gentle and placid in his way became more and more like the grandfather such that he wanted to be the one who was right (neither did the lay assessor in his time have an unruly or obstinate manner but he needed to be right, right no matter what, for what wouldn't one pay for domestic peace): but in the very middle of this was a gnawing, grinding doubt – did the others exist, was there more than a soft echoing emptiness, how was God's voice so distant that it only reached him as wrath and absence? A full long life of absence from one's self? And now here too walked Albert, a shifting shadow of himself, the shadow of everything in his life that was darkness and nothingness. Pale, heavy, confused. Even as an adult he would burst into tears over nothing.

Judit was showing herself to be the truly sharp and decisive one, the strongest in the family. When she finally got around to developing and matured fully – at the age of sixteen – she was as tall as her father; she worked more than all the others put together, and it became ever more apparent that she was waging a battle against him. Where, in her opinion, he was wasteful, she fought to collect, keep: she put out of sight, she locked away, she falsified weights and accounting ledgers. She battled silently and bone-hard, she battled for life. Fighting like this, not for herself but for them all, this was what she had taken upon herself, the task she never for a moment lost sight of. She did not rest. Rest was a thing that would have to come later, much later, when the task had been completed. When life had indeed finally been brought into safe haven with all its difficulty and uncertainty – then one could begin to think of rest. Not before.

Albert on the other hand did rest. He had days where he was in some way gone, then he'd so often have bad headaches; he couldn't work much. But when he was in good form he was willing if clumsy – he had to constantly be told what to do and how, he couldn't take things into his own hands. And he had a hard time getting things done albeit he did what he could. But Judit found it natural that she was the one who worked the most, she'd never thought otherwise: she worked, she made decisions and took on responsibility. More and more she did this. For with time it would also be her will that triumphed over her father though he didn't notice – he aged and become absent, thinking all the while that he was the one in charge (or perhaps it only mattered to him not to tear into the matter, to let it go, perhaps even with secret relief). There no longer came to the farm so many seeking help, he didn't think about it, assumed there were fewer people out there nowadays – he was unaware of how many Judit had driven away and of how word had spread in the area that it was now the daughter, the Queen, who was in charge of the farm, it wasn't easy to pass through the gates these days, help and hospitality couldn't be expected like before.

And she became the one to raise the youngest – with the heavy hand of a strict father. The father himself rarely spoke to him, avoided looking at him – the boy was so unlike them all, like a wild offshoot – when the father spoke to the children it was to the two eldest, at first under the pretext that the little one was too little and couldn't understand. Keeping him in check fell entirely to Judit: she had the strength for it: he was intractable as a child and this didn't abate as he grew, one must be strong, stronger than him, and resolutely patient to be able to control him. He'd grown differently than the two older ones, smaller but more composed and broad and strong and red in the face – due to blood and a boiling lust for life one imagined for he was on the go from morning to night, running, climbing, riding on cows, was all but a heap of dung come evening, he made life difficult for the person who was to keep him clean and whole. But in reality the color in his face came from an exceptionally fine and thin skin that let the blood shine clearly through, a weak and thin and easily wounded skin. And the whole of him was like this: apparent raw strength, full of reckless power like a small bull, trampling everything under foot – and he was, but also: easily harmed. And one never knew what might sting: it could be the sort of thing one was least likely to imagine, the sort of thing that truly in and of itself was nothing. Things struck and struck deep, where one would never have imagined a weak point to be. And he also had his very own sharp gaze, a repellent gaze; it was difficult to make sense of, it instilled insecurity, he was perhaps also insecure in himself, insecure down to his depths – the remarkable glittering pale eyes as if their slits were filled with rushing shining water or a kind of thick flickering light.

He respected Judit, for her strong hands perhaps – but because he too was growing and became equally strong, one could see it was not her limb strength that made it so, if that were the case she wouldn't have been able to maintain the upper hand for long, and yet she was stronger than many men. But no, it wasn't her physical strength, it was Judit herself. He never crossed her. He crossed everyone else with the full extent of his energy and ingenuity. But with Judit there was a boundary: she was stronger. Before her he stood red and dark of face and mute. His hands fisted, to be sure. But mute. And so she said a few words – she did not argue for long, not with many words. But he stood there and his tongue could not muster a single sound in reply. So she sent him away. And he went.

So she raised him, hard and strict, for she had a dream – she was raising him so that one day he would enter into the dream, he would become strong and hard. He would not be like their father, not be like Albert. No, he would be of help to her and a support, together they would restore the farm, together they would pull it up out of the endless viscous morass of debt. It was for this that she raised him. They were to work together and he would be her help in all things, her support. In this dream their parents were already gone. Albert was also elsewhere. The Queen and Viktor would live there together, together they would raise up the farm, they would always be together. For this she raised him. But for this he needed to be strong. And she raised him hard and strict and mercilessly stalked all that seemed weak and frail in him, Viktor was not permitted any weaknesses.

But the lament and piteousness would have their outlet somewhere. The lament and misery were inside him, he was in himself weak, not strong – so they came out transformed. And he revived himself with Albert. The little one spared his brother no provocation. He was like a stingfly buzzing around him – incessantly, incessantly. And some do know exactly where a sting will smart most.

Now it was true that Albert was a slow and indecisive sort on the inside as well, he had a difficult time arriving at what he actually thought and felt. Had a difficult time feeling at all – at least specific, articulated, clear feelings, what he felt always lay so deep, hard to reach, hidden down there in a formless rocking and billowing pale gloom (something like intestines or living dung). Between himself and what was down there was an unpleasant dullness, dense whitish, a fog or a billowing weave of membrane. For a long time he had no sense of the feelings he might have for his little brother. He thought for a long time that he liked him – as one likes or at least tolerates someone smaller and lacking in sense. Not much by way of feeling. But in any case. The only curious thing was that on this point he would fall silent inside: dead silent. The little one yowled (from a safe distance behind the water barrel by the henhouse) disguising his voice to mimic the girls' squeaking schoolyard taunt:

lard-butt-lard-butt-Albert-Albert-lard-butt –

This too Judit had endured.

She, the Queen.

And all fell silent inside him. No wrath, not a trace of wrath. It was just that everything inside him held its tongue. A stiff unclear strange silence reigned. Like an unmoving bank of clouds was he. And thereby something that toppled like dark knots of snakes. And he didn't know what he thought of his little brother, he told himself: it will improve with time. Yes. Yes. With time he will improve. Grow out of this – yes.

Albert was seventeen years old, heavy, large, wordless. Sometimes he would set off into the open land to be none but himself at a good distance from the farm. The world had this hollowness of betrayal – a ball of ice in his gut impossible to be rid of, impossible to forget, he fell asleep with it, when he woke up it was still there: the betrayal.

And the loneliness was difficult. It was a knot, a cramp. So he went into the heather, there was a pit of gray sand, fine cold sand, there one could lie down unseen, the heather provided cover. This was the locus of impurity. And he lay there on this back moaning with shame, a quiet quaking yammer that surged and sank in stiff waves, steps of a sleepwalker, mechanical.

One day the little one came upon him thus: he almost trod on him for all the heather hiding that overturned body. For a moment the little one stared uncomprehending down at the body where a patch of belly shone weak and white in the gap of his opened shirt, head flung-back, larynx working – a long moment, and at first couldn't comprehend that this was his brother, it seemed impossible to connect his brother to this other who lay there overthrown in the sand beneath tufts of heather: the body there in the sand tensed with ever greater force, from shoulder to loins it was almost like a bow arching into the loose sand. The heather was redolent. It was a gray damp day. The heather was luminous. The little one's eyes watched the body in the sand, how it quaked, how it shook, how it heaved from side to side as if steered by no one, a curious dead object brought to swing and swinging and swaying ever faster, in a void, without resistance. There came a final jolt as if the body at last managed to lift (or shake off) an intolerable burden; and the child saw how at once it was drained of power, all tension eased, releasing into a long sobbing sigh. Now the body that was his brother lay dead in the sand. The heather was redolent. The sea was redolent. A swarm of seagulls rose up screeching in a whirling gleam of wings into the gray. That long heavy body lay open in a stare of utter defenselessness

– weak, vulnerable, unguarded. Like a newborn before its limbs have had a chance to gather themselves from the haze, from the tight grip of birth's whirl – before the first movement, before the limbs draw together to protect themselves, before the first cry, the spasmodic scream. And the face to the sand was blurred, as if stripped, expressionless: heavy, vague, gray like a water-washed stone. Eyes shut.

The little one stood unmoving, was already mid-jump away.

Then Albert opened his eyes. And saw him.

His eyes were still and dark. They saw the little brother, his tormentor. And his eyes now reflected a nameless mull of horror.

The Queen ruled over them.

The little one grew up. Now he was already far too large for Judit to bathe him as she used to in the evenings, in the large zinc tub – this was already a distant memory, how she would wash his red rugged little body, not soft and rounded like a young child's usually is but like a small man's body, hard and warm with robust movements. Now he was big: eleven, twelve. And it was going as poorly in school as ever. Viktor learned to read at long last and with great difficulty, even in the third grade he was far from confident, and with the reading being so difficult he fell behind in everything else of course, he was forever facing an immovable gray pile, all that was unread and impossible to understand, it turned him refractory and mean, he was as restive as a yearling with anything related to school (for by nature he wished to be foremost, adversity did him no good, it distorted and diminished him, he couldn't bear it). And there were continual fights and stories and complaints; he had gotten off on the wrong foot from the start, one thing drew with it another, it was inevitable. There'd been an unspeakable dirty word carved into the surface of a desk (at this the father white-lipped pulled out his strap: You've brought shame upon me! You've brought shame upon me!). And windowpanes shattered one by one, focused, methodically. And newspaper-wrapped excrement in the teacher's drawer. And once he set upon a little boy in the first grade and pushed him over in the schoolyard planting his face in the dirt and rubbing it around until the boy wasn't screaming anymore – like a madman. For a very long time the first-grader's face was one single great sore. On this occasion his mother, she with dark hair, had to emerge from her absence and trudge the path of apology: yes you see we don't understand – it's as if something flies into him we don't understand – . It was Judit who forced her to do this. His father sat at the kitchen table: I want nothing to do with this. He is not my son anymore. He is not my son. His mother came home in tears. The things they'd told her about Viktor. They hadn't softened the edges. But truly what reason did they have to soften them? She looked at the boy who sat red in the corner where the stove was, stubbornly staring out at the farm, out into the gray dusk. He who was strange. Had he said a word. No apology would have been needed – just a simple word, anything. But he said nothing. And his mother's crying ceased, she fell silent and turned inward again. Through the dusk the lot of them saw the boy's glittering gaze over by the stove. The father turned his face away and stared out the window in the direction of the sea.

In the heavy gray silence they heard Judit draw a deep breath, her teeth met with a soft clack, but they did not continue to chatter, she clenched them and her eyes stayed clear and dry. She stood up, walked over to Viktor and struck him right in the face with full force. With this he began to cry and wrapped his arms around her and buried his face into her rough apron-clad chest. The father stood up as well, impossible to say if he was relieved or something else for he kept his face turned away: he walked quickly outside. Judit watched him walk across the farmyard to the gate from her place at the kitchen window with her brother close by: he was crying and shaking and pressing up against her, he was holding onto her so tightly, as if she were the last thing he could cling to – while something inside him sucked and pulled and wanted to draw him down to it. Judit's dry dark eyes followed their father – go on, go, you-betrayer. Go on, abandon us! And she pressed the brother to her and rocked him and spoke slowly, slowly to him. She then sensed that she was speaking to someone who could not defend himself. And she sensed that whatever happened she must believe this to be true.

Judit was now a young woman who in her way was beautiful with her large sharp pale face under a dark crown of hair, her deep-set eyes seemed dark too but were in fact gray – eye-stones the clarity of which is revealed as firelight falls through them, clear as the sea.

She'd grown tall, straight-backed and strong: she wasn't afraid of anything and she was stronger than many men – it was said that she could take a stubborn steer by the horns and bend its head down until it relented. Such was the perception of her strength. She was of course beautiful in her way, but her way didn't seem to bring men around to thoughts of love for her: strong, strict, taciturn (unless it regarded her youngest brother), beautiful in her way, she walked there; no, the thought was unthinkable, who would have dared? She was enough in and of herself – whole, sufficient. Not that she didn't sense her sex, to the contrary it was strong and clear within her, but it was precisely that it was so clear and limited in how it could be perceived, strong and tormenting and foreseeable. It was a thing in her self, a superficial thing, a soulless thing, in it she perceived herself, but it wasn't something she perceived other beings, men, with. In this way she was closed off and not to be broken open: she was in and of herself enough. Her weak spot was the boy, Viktor, this was the only place through which things could penetrate, anything to do with him touched her deep inside, cut a path to the core, harming, wounding – and someone in her, a hidden being, hungered and thirsted to be broken apart, harmed in this way as well. Her brother, her child, lived at the very center of her heart, in every moment her body and soul perceived his existence. This brother, her child, was the only surety in all that was shifting – for with the farm it was impossible to look ahead, impossible to know if it would still be there in a few years (or next year even); with the father and money it was a like a quagmire.

She and her brother, the child was the only thing that was fitting and proper, the world around was empty, sick, but between her and this brother flowed real, living, nourishing blood: from her to him, from him to her. Together they were going to take the farm.

And sometimes in those rare moments that she happened to be sitting still (she was otherwise on the go from the dawn to the dark night) she could perceive in her arms and hands the living weight and heat of the swaddled child from before. His tender bare red head rested heavy on her arm – she saw it so clearly almost like a vision. And she bent toward the tender hot face to feel the skin, the hot breath; then he opened his eyes and she looked right into their curious shimmering pallor and for a moment it was as if she would be torn from herself (like a soundless storm a tree from the earth roots and all), he rested there in her arms with wide-open eyes, but as she was about to touch her lips to his forehead – nothing was there. She sat there arms empty, breasts empty. Outside the window the great bare meadows down by the sea. She was overcome with terror: was anything real?

But she and him – that was a surety. The world was full of misfortune, each farm had its share. But this was a sure thing, after all she had raised him herself, he was a part of her.

And she ruled over him. And he was to obey. Thus she knew that she herself existed, that he existed. She ruled. Thus it became real.

But things happened.

The first of them happened just after Viktor turned seventeen. Around that time the father had begun to decline, went silent and white, it took ever longer for him to dress himself, bring a cup to his mouth, go out into the house – him going out into the fields, Judit discovered in the month of November, was suddenly out of the question, not possible. How long had it been since he'd been beyond the courtyard? Several months, in fact, since he even talked about getting outside, it must have been soon after the harvest in the short break before the start of the autumn work, that he suddenly gave up. For she remembered him at the harvest, snow-white within his beard, cold-sweating in the blazing sun, he did what he was supposed to, but the whole time those with him were wondering at which moment he'd fall to the ground. He did not fall, he did not complain, but at the slightest mention of his health, that he should spare himself, he was beside himself – for the first time in his life he dug his heels in with his work, impossible to get him away from it; when exhaustion finally forced him inside (but never before the others) fear burst into his gaze, for a moment his eyes were so wide-open and helpless none could bear to meet them. But after the harvest he gave out: by the time the leaves began to fall he'd given up, now his life was that of an invalid, he did not speak of it but he knew it. There was snow as early as Christmas; it was a joyless Christmas. And Judit had then also begun to ask herself in earnest what was going on with Viktor: he slunk in the corners, looked no one in the eye. The first work day after New Year's she was in the store, she'd arrived early and found herself alone with the shopkeeper's wife who did not mince words when informing her of what the whole area was buzzing about: that Viktor had made the Landö lighthouse keeper's daughter pregnant and the girl was already in her seventh month. She was thin and frail (Judit, by the way, was well aware of her appearance) and that belly she'd grown could be spotted from a mile off.

The Queen took her goods and left.

This is what one looks like when one has lost one's crown. Gray. Poor.

Judit drove home thus, the reins in her slack hands and the horse striding as it pleased through the slush, sometimes it stopped and turned its head and gave her a questioning look. But it was as if she'd been dealt a blow to the head, time had stopped for her, only after a long while did she wake up, then she drove into her own farm. The horse stopped of its own accord at the gate. She sat a while on the cart. It was such a long while that her head began to droop to her chest. But she did not cry, her gaze was large and tearless. A snowy haze shrouded the world, all was close and silent. After a while she gave herself a shake, climbed down and began with slow dead movements to unharness the horse.

But the matter resolved itself, a few weeks later the lighthouse keeper's daughter fell through a small hole in the ice, she floated up farther down the coast but only after several weeks.

In the time when the lighthouse keeper's daughter was missing but not yet found, Judit came upon Viktor one day, he was standing in the north chamber which was clad in black-and-gold wallpaper, to look upon it was as if to enter an Eden of gold – there he stood, his finger following the curious flowers' journeys into each other. The soft groan of the door opening made him flinch and look up – there they stood face to face, and never had she seen a face so naked and exposed, it was as if the skin had been torn from it, and his eyes were full of a helpless despairing wild fear. They stood like that a moment, looking at each other. Then the Queen walked out.

Later the lighthouse keeper's daughter was found. And the whole winter through, far out on the snowy expanse her grave shone brown and freshly cleared of snow, the cemetery's gentle slope lay in plain sight on the very edge of that rise of land.

And most in these parts now hardened their faces and fell silent when Judit arrived, everyone made it clear that no more talk of her distinct and distinguished brother would be tolerated.

And they did not forgive in these parts.

And Viktor's face, his eyes, were full of fear.

And after a while something hard and contracted appeared, but it was as if his face was forever on the verge of breaking.

And after a short time the Queen had occasion to say that (albeit sheer madness) Viktor was undoubtedly cooking up something new, this time with Agnes Erlandsson from the first farm in Bäck. She was gray and fat, and Viktor went around with a mocking mien as if he wanted to contest that he was doing this in order to vex, only to vex.

But their parents perceived none of this. For the father slowly week by week was ever more quickly moving toward death. And the mother was bound to him – not in love, it did not in any way resemble love, but in the way that whatever may happen, whatever you want for yourself, you're bound to your body.

In the midst of it all spring arrived nonetheless. Spring came early that year, by the middle of February the snow had already gone and it did not return. A few sunny biting fresh storm days came; with them the ice dispersed and the lighthouse keeper's daughter's hole in the ice was gone (they'd found her basket and gloves next to the hole, from which they surmised that this was the hole that belonged to her, to her death), the sea lay open and blindingly blue-black, the swans glided snow-white across the dark blue but not a single ice floe remained. The sedge stood pale yellow and dead, its tinder-dry rustle in the soft sunny breeze the day after the storm, the swells heaved still and icy in the blue. The juniper and hawthorn shone red along the sea road which after the snowmelt was but a mud-dark bottomless wheel-track.

The long doleful frost-cool blue dusk in the time of the snowmelt. The blackbird's fluting in the garden. Her limbs felt weary, searingly heavy. Why won't he come? What is he doing now?

For it was as if the whole world had betrayed them. As if the solid ground had shifted and become otherwise.

As if a deep maw leading all the way to the underworld had opened up on the ordinary smooth road: as if the road leading to the large road, the village road where she knew every stone and tree and willow shrub by the roadside, the village road that had been as identical and unchanged in her memory for as long as she could recall – as if a furious ravine had opened up in it devouring trees, bushes, rocks, cattle: as if the plains, all that was familiar had been broken up, become new, terrible.

It was as if there were destruction within him. Harrying.

It was as if this were a matter of upsetting everything for the sake of something he then couldn't be bothered with. He opened the cupboard and stuffed himself with sugar, all the while stealing glances at Judit expecting an outburst – for sugar was among the things she counted and weighed after she'd cut it, and then this precious item was doled out among them one carefully measured piece at a time, having more than one piece being the most sinful waste of all; she held fast to this.

But sugar is sugar. Human beings are another matter.

And this Agnes was hardly as alluring as a piece of white sugar – large and lumpy, beautiful teeth but her skin was gray and pimpled. And now Judit had Agnes in her kitchen the whole day long, she took any excuse to visit, and her large gray body radiated. And her beautiful teeth, small and clear as milk teeth, could be glimpsed in her loose half smile, like the sudden flash of pebbles in a marshy gray bed of sand when met by the sun. That gray body believed itself to be loved. But this was not so, it was otherwise. And nothing is more risible than someone who believes themselves to be loved but is in fact mistaken, she who believes herself to be alone and protected in the secret of her love, enfolded in its heat, but eyes from every direction see her, those laughing take pleasure in her heavy, ridiculous fumbling movements – from every direction she is observed, from every direction eyes glitter, from every direction soundless shaking laughter.

How could life be so risibly desecrated. Of a sudden. It had been great and earnest. And then. Maimed, hard pressed. A twisted stinking rag, sparse drops of watery rotten blood: the smell of dead blood drives the soul into corners from which it defends itself like an ailing rat soundlessly gasping hissing mad with fear and rage.

Thus the spring wears on, farthest in the corner on the settle in twilight (resting neck against the wall and staring down across meadows, sea) is the father's death-marked face. Viktor sits across from him and bites his nails and doesn't look at his father and not at the Queen: forced to play prosecutor (prosecutor even in that screaming dream, the white stiff dead one who comes to tie him to a table, the prosecutor, the whole court and the panel of lay assessors behind his back), Viktor stares sullenly into himself, impossible to catch his gaze, it's as if the light has gone out of it, withdrawn – the father doesn't look at his son either, he endures this child's presence, no more; soon he will die after all, what has grown wrong stays wrong, too late to put such things right.

Spring wears on: the chestnut's thick sticky brown buds burst their scales one day and frail green leaves unfurl, the greenery is lush and fragrant, the evenings go white as glass and the chestnut flowers light their dark-white spires within the damp deep green tree-darkness, from the willow shrubs the nightingales sound, however long night wears on darkness does not come, they sing and darkness does not come, the night keeps watch as white, as fragrant, quiet, sleepless – at this the madness rises like a fire inside her:

Crush it. Crush it.

But she is Queen after all, she is practiced in keeping her face stiff and unmoving, she has had plenty of time to prepare herself. She is queen after all. And now the Queen's moment has come: triumph or rupture.

The Queen does triumph, after all nothing else can be, her limbs wrap themselves like a stone around what's burning, the burning movements, the flaming face that wants to push forth from the stone. The fire is stifled, after all nothing else can be, but fire that is stifled where does it go, where on earth does it spread?

And once in the hot gray May twilight she saw under the hedge the beast with two backs, a mirage perhaps.

Then one day she asked him to drive up to the store. It was nothing out of the ordinary. But he said: no. And again he said: NO!

Eventually he was standing close to her and simply screaming, that is to say the air hissed from his throat powerlessly pulsing: Go to hell! Go to hell! And he spat right in her face. And he stood unmoving, simply staring. And his face twitched, around his mouth (well yes, she knew, she *knew* that this was a child about to burst into tears, but why could she no longer reach the child, why was this so, long ago she touched the child's cheek and mouth, whence came this rock-hard awful closure?).

And he walked off.

And she stood there. The Queen. There went what was alive in her – away. And she stood like an unmoving shadow in the kitchen, raised hand to cheek: shadow and stone, gust and wail. She sensed this was her death.

But as if under a stone she was dreaming, the obscure in her was dreaming:

Someone spoke: "Thus thou knowest a child of love is born obscure."

She wondered who it was who was speaking in this manner. Then she saw her brother's face heave past her as if on a wave, contorted, open mouth, eyes shut. As if he were dead in the sea, carried up and over high white-frothing waves – but he was not dead, from pate to sole this sleeping body sensed: he is not dead. Skin quaking, his face was above her. It was her youngest brother's face.

And she called out in her dream.

– but her voice didn't make it, it died on its way, and sweetness, such sweetness burst forth from her heart. Not from the limbs. From the heart, from what is hidden. Clear as water, pure, dark, unforeseen.

And she woke up and she lay there looking into the dawn – it was the white fragrant dawn – and pure deep strong joy filled body and mind to the brim, all was alive: all was joy. Long she lay like this and barely dared breathe so as not the disrupt this mysterious joy. It was the fragrant white dawn in the month of June. All was as it should be. All was as it only could be. Was she mother, was she sister, was she wife? All was as it only could be.

But thereupon was daylight. And the Queen was in possession of her vision, of her senses, the Queen did not see her brother's face, the Queen was caged in her senses as if in garb of stone, as if cast in stone; she saw only the young male body walking there, moving; the Queen stared, looking out from her burning stone prison; and as she couldn't get free, as she could only see a body moving, heavy, hot, she took to hating; and she hated him such that she felt her skin burning and quaking with hatred; she felt her hands ball into fists, the Queen's strong hands they wanted to kill and to perceive death.

Judit sensed the Queen triumphing, now she has me by the throat, now my limbs will turn to stone, my hair writhing stone snakes, gaping stone mouth, bulging great empty stone eyes. The fire has passed through the stone, the stone became radiant with fire, the fire blazed on, the stone extinguished. The fire has made me eternal. Now I have in my stone body a stone heart. The Queen has me, I am queen of myself, in the land of twilight I am left to eat stone.

And one day when she looked upon her youngest brother she felt that her gaze had also changed. She sensed how it had become indifferent in a way. It fell upon all else, it fell upon him, there was no difference. At once nothing he did affected her, there was no change for the better, it was as if all had been emptied of life, what could now remain? And she started to say to him that the likes of him would never survive over in the States – not that she wanted him gone exactly, she did want and did-not-want, but she told herself that it was for his sake, he would be forced to pull himself together over there.

In some way she'd imagined that he'd take off when their father went into the long night. And by that time everything would be arranged: purged.

But she did not see the confusion in his rough helpless face. And she didn't see how the child in him was fumbling for help.

The Queen was consumed by her own pain, from the walls of Jerusalem she stretched her pain out across the mountains, her heart cried out like a body about to be crushed under a boulder, if the weight of death is not lifted, if the bedrock does not shift, will she not crack?

No.

Deep inside there is crying, there is anguish.

But Judit is already dead, long dead: walking around, moving, seeing and hearing, but like one dead.

He was fumbling around. There was also his mortal fear of the impending military service, all he embarked upon called up misfortune like a current that catches at the bottom dredging up seaweed and rope mussels entwined with all manner of detritus, a great dark tangle of the unforeseen suddenly lands in the boat, thus all he did dredged up misfortune (far too much misfortune for the wretched little he'd done, truly, he thought), misfortune surrounded him, it was the world, the mother water, misfortune was around him like a dark still water, it was essential not to move, not to breathe in, not to swallow because then it would get inside them, it was already bad at home but beyond the home he dared not imagine, he certainly did not dream of the States, Viktor, as having to do his military service in Ljungbyhed was enough of a nightmare. And whatever he embarked upon he brought with him one dead, two counting the unborn child she'd carried with her into death, they were his invisible companions, vanguards rather – for whatever he did, whoever he wanted to reach he had to pass by them first, the lighthouse keeper's daughter and the one unborn.

From the start to go around as if in the kingdom of the dead. Life began in the kingdom of the dead, there he was joined and betrothed after all. (deep from below, deep below, came the gentle enticing call, out of the dusky unseen like the fluting trills of a female thrush)

But the Queen did not see. The Queen saw herself.

The father now lay in bed for good. The summer grew hot. In August all the grass burned up, brown. Often he didn't have the energy to keep himself clean, they had to wash him and change him. His gaze was often glassy, stiff, distant: he didn't hear, didn't react. Was like a thing.

One day Judit was washing him. She noticed he was developing bed sores – dark holes of early rot the size of apples. Still not-much dissolved. But a weeping start. She could feel how her face stiffened, shut itself, but she managed to control herself, she did not dash for the door. Still something about her must have altered, perhaps her hands became twitchy, harder, for he woke from his half-slumber and for a moment – a long moment – he looked at her with full alive, dark, clear recognition. He mumbled something – she bent down: did he want something?

No, no the Queen heard him whisper. It's you – about you –

He paused, the only sound was the buzzing of flies in the afternoon heat, his breath was labored and uneven.

You want such big things, he mumbled, again on his way out.

– but what will be our salvation is a meagre thing that crushes no one – crushes not a single one of us –

With this he'd lost his thread again, his mouth lost itself in sound, bubbling saliva. She dried his chin and helped him lie back on the pillow. Then she fetched salve and talc for the sores. And she controlled herself. But she could not help despising him. Where he lay (and now with what was weeping and dissolving) he was her confirmation. He'd been wrong. And now he was in dissolution, from within. So it was.

He'd been wrong, the Queen said to her mother and Albert. And so it went as it went. Things would be different now.

(– but Viktor? –)

– extinguished blood, blackening meadows, thistle shafts seeding silvery death. A death as light as frost after all breathing in the universe stopped: the sky white and stiff, the sea spread white as a fever-soaked sheet gone cold.

The linen sheet, to the dying one the wedding sheet. Autumn is coming. Carline thistle and thorn apple seed death. Still, still. The universe empty above the sea.

He gets up from the settle bed, shirt wound around him like a wet wrinkled rag, they cannot hold him, his chest, its tufts of hair sweat-damp, lifts and sinks as if being beaten by a hammer – as if heavy resonant hammer blows were strike by strike pressing him from within and outward, out of himself, the dull blows are at work, the mouth gapes dark and open with its rotten tooth stumps, his large eyes shine bulging for once wide-open (otherwise they've always lain half-hidden deep under soft-wrinkled eyelids), a call presses forth from his chest, by fits, hoarse, they can no longer hold him, he is screaming like an animal.

Unmoving the Queen looked down upon this obscure person's struggle with death. Anxious eyes, blood-tinged mucus in the mouth, mortal body wheezing and leaking and creaking like an old ship the moment before the joins give way, each truss breaks, all is scattered. Jesus Christ our savior, quaked the mother's feeble voice by the headboard. Yes, he lay there before them on the settle bed in the north chamber with the gold wallpaper and he lay there dying, there was no doubt about it.

Then they heard him call to Viktor.

And Viktor was present, he flung himself down beside the settle and rested his head on his father's chest: indeed, Viktor was present. But his father did not recognize him, the father's eyes were directed elseward and death anxiety continued to pierce the air with its shrill voice: But my child! Dear child where are you, where are you?

Viktor was kneeling there by him, crying and quaking. But father did not recognize son.

Then Judit caught sight of his hands.

For as his eyes were staring and seeking, his dark yellow large gnarled old hands took hold of his son's shoulders, those hands were no longer searching, they'd found but they were no longer able to formulate what they had found, the dying man no longer perceived them, he was elseward, from within a darkness he was searching and calling out in anguish for a child he'd abandoned there once many years ago. And he could not find him.

Thus he died and was buried. Viktor wanted no part in the funeral, neither did he come along, they could not persuade him – when it came to the moment after the great door had been flung open and before the coffin was to be carried out, he was not present. He was simply not there. Gone. He fled to the woods, or rather to the heath – later they'd hear that he'd been spotted upon the heath, he'd wandered there the whole day through, reclining in heather and broom, eating nothing, drinking nothing. Meanwhile the father was buried. Judit the Queen stood tall, large and white, dressed in black by the open grave, staring out over the gray meadows beyond the wall. Standing by the low bank of shoveled earth around the hole of the grave Albert read aloud, his eyes turned to the gray heat-hazed August sky, "on behalf the relatives" . . . "for I know that my redeemer liveth." After that it was done. Late into the dark fragrant hot evening steps upon the gravel path were heard. The Queen looked out. Then the lighthouse beacon shone. Its light caught Viktor standing on the path, unmoving caught in the light, in dusty disheveled clothes, his raised-up face was white, sweaty, ruined.

And afterward it was simply such that the Queen could no longer control Viktor. He did as he pleased, came as he pleased, went as he pleased – even when things were at full tilt. Especially then, it seemed to the Queen. She sat there, fretting. They were now engaged in a battle between life and death.

Albert, however, did obey. And the Queen recovered him. Sent him here. Sent him there. The Queen had a stiff dead face, her desire was to reign. But he did also seem to enjoy being obedient.

But she felt a disgust for this obedient personage, as for a body without bones, weak, gristly.

But for Albert the Queen was to be endured like life was to be endured, in reality this person was of course not Judit, the real Judit was someone he once knew long ago (it was getting to be quite a while ago now) the real Judit had been exchanged. And now wore a disguise. And all he could do was wait and endure until this Queen cracked and fell away, the Queen was not real, she was a dead harbor, at some point she would have to be delivered and the real one would emerge once more. All there was to do was wait. Now was the time of wandering in the desert. But at some point this must end. And then they would be together again on those green meadows (with the great effervescent fresh sea beyond), then the lifeless soundless empty desert would simply begin to fade like the memory of thirst.

But time passed. Life kept on its way, it continued, nothing changed. Judit stayed the same, no one in these parts called her anything but Queen, even Reverend Bergenstråhle in Ljungby had once accidentally addressed her as such; when she was coming tall dark and strong one felt from a distance that this was the Queen in Bäck, the Queen battled against the bank, her large beautiful face hardened in its features, grew paler, they'd been adults for a long time now, were already deep into adult life. It didn't get better. Despair began to drill its way up, taking ever more space inside him, had the real Judit perhaps never existed? Had this person only been a dream he'd had. At some point in the darkest corner of the attic in the aroma of flour (but the rats! the rats' eyes!) when he'd been sitting there sucking his fingers.

Someone in him told him to believe in the good Judit, whatever may come. The Queen had locked away the good Judit. In a pit the good Judit lay wounded, he could not stop believing in her even if his entire life so passed without him ever glimpsing her again, he could not abandon her.

Thus time went by. Viktor went to do his military service and returned; he returned and his face was hard, now he refused to let himself be caught in a moment of secret weakness, he refused to let any hidden fear be seen by others, he'd learned something during his service. Their mother died and was laid beside their father in the grave. Viktor had returned and knew he was not welcome, now he'd learned to drink and gamble, he lived a fast life that the two striving on the farm could only grasp in incomprehensible flashes, better to shield your eyes from that sort of thing. The Queen bemoaned the youngest to whoever would listen, there was hatred in her voice such that it almost seemed to corrode her lips. A time of crisis came, the long heavy years wore down their stamina and energy, they hadn't needed this on top of all else. The Queen had a truly difficult time making ends meet. And she would not take to the black market in the city. Everyone else could. But not her. She simply would not. It hardly made her likable in these parts, people thought it was as if she were setting herself above them and judging them, that she thought herself better and above the misery and hardships of common people. And she did. She thought about her lily beds as she walked the furrows, bellowing at the horses like a man, she dreamed that one day the master gardener at Trolle Ljungby castle would bespeak her bulbs, a dream that never came true.

But the Queen had what belonged to her, something kept her earth-bound, there was always something for her to swallow down, this issue with Victor and women – with his reputation he would inevitably be blamed for all the fatherless children born in these parts. (And the Queen did pay, without a word, it was too embarrassing to touch with words, to dispute and haggle over – no one could prove it so or otherwise; but there were a few gray loose girls, with uncertain faces, uncertain conduct, who came creeping to demand paternal maintenance, they even kept coming when he was far away, over in the States, and she could not protest.)

But there was no question about one child. It had been born in Torp across the heath. And however it was with the other children, this one was at least last in the line. After this one Viktor did not engage with another woman while he was still living at home.

There was no question that this child was his but they were not permitted to pay for her, unlike the others. Not even an öre. And for this child's upkeep he would have gladly paid dearly, gladly paid with his whole life. But he was not permitted. Such was the matter:

One day Viktor saw a girl on the road. She was a tall, straight-backed, strong girl, with an earnest face and a dark crown of hair, moreover there was delicacy to her, she held her head high – unlike others. Viktor saw her. And it took but a moment for him to feel that the only thing of importance in life was to have this girl, if he could have her his life would become life, if he could not it would be over.

He saw that even for a person in a kingdom of death there was a flaming and burning and youthfully scented hope in life. And it was a matter of life to reach her.

He found out from where she hailed – from upon Torp across the heath.

At the depths of sleep and waking she was. He roved like a madman – in joy, in anguish. Imagine that such a thing was possible.

But the girl wanted nothing to do with him.

But whatever the case he succeeded in forcing his way to her and forcing himself upon her; he called out loudly that she was his life, his only treasure, the only joy his eyes had ever known; but she wanted nothing to do with him; whatever the case – he did not take her by force, not exactly, but it was still in great confusion and against her will that the girl gave herself. And when she saw the crying blazing face over her she understood that she'd caused damage that could not be repaired. It happened a few times, not many – she understood that this could not continue, all of it was fallacious, without future. She was seized by an ever-deeper loathing for herself and him. And when she found herself with child, she loathed him even more, she couldn't even stand the sight of him. He arrived with an offer of marriage but she had her brothers drive him out the gate – they were singular people up in Torp, not like others, the parents had this girl last of all when they were already quite old, now the father was dead, but for the mother and the brothers she was the jewel of their eye. She was their queen, whatever she did was to them correct. And it was correct in its way: she was stately and straight and singular, she was on her own path, and it she followed. And she walked upon the heath expecting her child, Christmas Eve 1917 she gave birth to a girl, and her mother and brothers and she herself received the little one and delighted in her as one does in a gift from God, something beyond words. But Judit knew that as soon as the opportunity presented itself Viktor would be roaming the heath near Torp, he'd be circling the farm like a wounded animal seeking a place of rest. But he was given none, he was not received. The child was over there in Torp, but he wasn't allowed to see her; he'd only seen her from a distance once or twice. Judit knew that the little one existed, but had yet to see her. After this ordeal Viktor lost his interest in women; but it was hard to say if this change was for the better, he drank even more, he was ever dark, threatening, half-drunk. In a way the Queen could see that in this he should not be judged. But she could not concede. So they went around barking at each other, day out, day in; it was as if their words of anger were how they came into contact, they couldn't help themselves. But one day, a good two years after this had happened, Judit went to the store. There stood an old straight-backed white-haired woman with a child, a girl child, on her arm; something rang out in Judit, hard to say if it was fear or a type of unfathomable happiness

– it was the old woman from Torp. The old woman looked her right in the eye without the slightest quiver in her own face that might betray a knowledge of who she was. But Judit was not looking at her, she was looking at the little one, she couldn't take her eyes off her. The child had a slender strong face, eyes set quite deep, in shadow but shining – she dimly reminded Judit of something, something with peculiar familiarity, like climbing into one's own skin, and suddenly she realized that the girl resembled her. She felt her knees buckle, she needed to go out to the porch. The vacant snow plain stared back at her. A weak damp gust came from the sea, it smelled of wrack and thaw. Briefly she rested her forehead against the porch post. It was as if her whole life had been sent spinning: very clearly she saw the child's narrow forehead and the dark hair falling toward her chin. Thereupon the old woman came out on the porch with the girl still on her arm, the shopkeeper followed behind and helped her stack and secure her goods on the kick-sledge, the little one sat atop the load, she had a shawl wrapped around her head and chest, under her shawl that dark hair lay against her chin. Then the grandmother drove off with her into the forest, toward the heath. The Queen stood on the porch and looked, looked.

But for Viktor it was as if he'd sunk into quicksand. Something gliding sucked, sucked. He wasn't human anymore. He sat in the kitchen, his intoxicated face gone dark, darkened shining eyes, drinking and drinking with dry mute lips.

And one day Viktor found that what remained for him was to take America. For years the Queen had been hoping it would come to this. Judit did not object, perhaps he'd imagined she would. But she did not object, it was a comprehensive solution after all; and what was said was as good as done, now it could not be changed; suddenly he was in the midst of travel preparations without actually having wanted this. It appeared to him that the Queen was going around smiling with hate: now we'll see. To be rid of him was to scrape the bottom. Even so, everything else to do with him had become so difficult that this in itself almost impossible matter of arranging the trip seemed to her surmountable.

And in this way it came to pass that one beautiful blustery September day at sunset, the year was 1920, Viktor Lindgren from Bäck in Ljungby in Sweden was standing on West 63rd Street in New York holding his suitcase in his hand, the rough stiff red hand whitened as it clutched the handle and he stared into the air in front of him, wondering in which direction he should go, up or down. For he was in the maelstrom. A mighty sea of people, of faces, welled forth, welled forth, they welled up out of howling caves, out of ash-black buildings, going up and down the roaring rattling iron stairs. Like the endless empty Atlantic when it darkens into night and becomes an icy torrent, he discovered that the great heaving wash of human mass had a direction, movements, faces, limbs, waves, factory whistles, the grating and moaning of buses braking, all was swept into a single sucking current – outward! outward! – black heavy stained surface with the angled sunbeams' (through the smoke haze, smoke wisp) cold red light on the faces surfacing through the darkness.

In the waves: in the waves the current mighty, suctioning, a drowse, a pull toward death. Every building wall strange. Every face unfamiliar, cold.

It was not from without that he perceived how he was losing his footing – from-outside-reality was real enough, the pitted torn-open patched-up asphalt, blinking signs, in an already illuminated window a cobbler was mending shoes with his quick lead hands, blue smoked from a kitchenette in the corner, two stocky men with gray skin were greedily and quietly eating fried fish off of greasy newspaper, smell of oil, smell of sweat, printer's ink, smoke, rotten lettuce, onion steam.

But from within.

As if deep from within, somewhere down on the very bottom, farther he could not go – he was being dissolved. Root fibers turned to slime, drifting lifeless into the dark. As the smallest child in the crowd of people surging down the street like a river runs through an endless ravine (neither did the street seem to have an end, it cut through the twilight all the way to ruddied evening sky, somewhere over there it was burning and the ravine's sweaty walls rose like fire-bright glass), mothers in dark musty clothing in alien cuts, Eastern Europe, the corridors of the Immigration Office were packed with such small-boned dark-haired gray-skinned beings, the bundles, children, laments, howls, white headscarfs, carrying in their arms infants that looked like dirty wads of cloth with small gray faces, holes for eyes. He could feel himself being dissolved. From within. From below. Darkness. Now he was but face and body. And he walked into a bar, there he took a room on the other side of the courtyard (a black well, it smelled of trash and rot, at the very top a patch of fire-sky the size of a fingernail) and poured into a mug of beer a foul tasting colorless liquor: was given more, got rowdy and rough, remembered later that he'd fought his way forward, to be given even more and more, hit someone, downed more, a stream of riled-up voices. He'd flown through the air. Darkly.

And of course he lost his wallet, money, and suitcase. Thus began Viktor Gustaf Lindgren's life in America.

He had set off to take America, to fight his way free by fighting his way forward. There in the unknown, in the free. There one could fall freely – in the direction a person so chose.

But could one fall in any way but eternally in the same direction? In any way but forever back down into one's self?

And it also became clear that America would only very slowly allow itself to be taken.

To be sure, he found work almost immediately. But it was unfamiliar and unpleasant work – with a demolition company, the lime dust made him break out in a rash, only Italians there, they kept their spaghetti-heat to themselves, he didn't understand them, not their language, not them. After a while he became a milk man: he drove around with horses and almost felt at home: but whatever the case the idea that America couldn't be conquered had been stamped on him, it is immense, cold, strange, it would have been different if there'd been a way back, if that had been possible to consider. But back was death. Beyond the Atlantic lay death. Everything that was back was impossible to touch even with the faintest of thoughts, it was poisoned, unbearably painful, a dead something inside him spread slow rot around itself so that the slightest gesture in that direction shot pain through to his fingertips. And he couldn't have anything to do with women anymore, the mere thought was impossible and ensconced by an anguish that made it feel like being stifled, cold sweat sprung forth, his larynx twitched. Sometimes he could clearly see what he'd become, a sort of mad or maimed man. And there was no way back. His only solace was the horses, large brown warm and good-natured, groom them, harness them, drive them, this was satisfaction, them he could caress without dread. There was no way back. But when his hand rested on their warm rump it recalled something that needed to stay in its place: as a soft strong heat in the palm. In this manner he lived on. Then he started driving a truck, he'd learned how, he moved over to a transport company, as a trucker he saw the eastern and southeastern states, mostly at nighttime. Then he eventually took up with womenfolk again – added up year on year (he drove for the company for six years) it was no small number. Still as if he'd had none at all. It was a terror. Terror could be driven out, broken, forgotten. To come so close it felt like nothing. In this fashion he moved forward between darkened limbs, faces gone dark – from body to face, the one more strange than the next, only the new strange blank faces could be endured; made the memories as heavy as gravestones – sunk them into oblivion, in deep water.

He drove for the company for six years. Then times worsened. One day he was fired. Just like that. And there he stood.

It was then as if he'd lost his footing. But after a while he said that he wanted to have a look around the country. He found a new job in Baton Rouge, Louisiana, Southern Express Co. The transports took place at night. But luck had now abandoned him, what would come to pass came to pass on the third night, it was also the case that in some way he'd begun to feel worried and worn-out, something was confused and muddled up inside him since that day he was suddenly standing on the street in New York – thrown out, just like that, after six years. On the third night God's hand caught up with him in the backwoods between Baton Rouge and Delacroix. This was all still part of the delta bayou: the road runs along a bank high above swamp and quagmire. Down on the sides simmering darkness, the truck's headlights bored into the night, meeting carrion encased in white mineral skin, perhaps a horse that had been pulled down and that the swampland was now returning with contorted limbs and a sunken belly covered with whitish, crystalline, light-catching salt deposits; the headlights sweeping through the dark that echoes and quakes like the skin of a drum with the ear-splitting mating song of the cajun chorus frog. Through the latticework and tunnels of foliage the sharp delimiting blinding white beam cut into a layer of darkness that had never before known light, the driver's burning eyes meet an incredible scene – the surface of the swampland's stagnant black water begins to glimmer like great clusters of crushed gems, scatters and chains of small ruby-glinting points paired up, two by two, thousands of pairs of red-shining frog eyes out of the hot dark mire (marsh gas, water bloom, rush, honey moth nests, small dead fish, a baby alligator with its ballooning pale belly in the air), thousands or hundreds of thousands of red points, the driver sees spreads of eyes, dead frightened, red – in that very moment he didn't just lose control of his truck, the heavy vehicle drove off the side of the road and somersaulted over the tall road bank. It landed on its roof ten meters farther down in the raucous engulfing swampland. The Swede didn't even lose consciousness, after a few moments, his whole body shaking, he was able to get out of the cab which was upside down, hood wedged into the mud. And the mud sucked and sucked, slowly but relentlessly. Towing the truck would be no easy matter. He made his way up to the road, now that the headlights had gone dark in the mud it was pitch dark, the darkness quivered and vibrated like a skin below the frog calls; all around he only glimpsed dark forest horizons against the faint shine of the starry sky; where it now lay, the truck was impossible to tow; all he could do was flee the state as fast as he could before the police and the company and the insurance man arrived, whatever the case the blame would fall on him.

And it was his to bear.

Whatever the case he knew unwaveringly that he was guilty.

It was as unavoidable as his own skin: he was guilty.

This was something he hadn't been aware of – as if the revolution that occurred when he was slung into darkness had shaken out a brand new person, one whom he'd previously only sensed in part: guilty.

But he did escape the state of Louisiana – night – a route that took him fourteen days. Some days and nights he lived in a half-slumber of bright false hopefulness: it'll work out – one day. But something had happened inside him. And everything now felt so arbitrary, arbitrary life, arbitrary death.

Back in New York he found no work. No work was to be found anymore.

The times got worse. Now the unemployed were mostly who one met. The long dark quiet lines. He came to know hunger – what hunger is like when it is old, rooted, when day builds upon day.

And one knows one has been conquered. And for that there is no cure. The cold wealthy facades were impregnable. They would survive. But he would sink to the bottom. The farther he slid (she wouldn't have recognized him, the Queen, the way he looked as one conquered: calloused and gaunt, the jut of his chin was pointy in a way that one would never have anticipated, eyes gleaming like a drunk) the farther he slid down into exhaustion, finding rest arbitrarily (park benches, warehouses, switchyards) the more clearly she emerged. (curious, it had been nine years –) The Queen, she got me in the end! And he felt in his famine haze how she was standing over him where he lay – where he lay so shrunken and gray, so unlike himself, the shadow of himself. She stood over him, she did not move, she was smiling. In this dream he murdered her.

But then something unexpected happened.

Thirty to fifty men were needed, it had been said. But when he arrived – early in the half-dark dawn – the large open space in front of the factory was already dark with people, men but also many women, new arrivals kept welling from the black gape of the stairs under the pale shining letters I.R.T. and the mass of people was thus also in constant motion, one could hear feet shuffling and shoe tacks scraping across the frost-hard ground – this was the only sound, a dense silence reigned. With each passing minute – it was still long until the clock would strike seven – the mass of people compacted, the number of tired tense faces compacted, they first appeared gray similar hushed dark faces of lead but the more it brightened the whiter they paled in the dawn's clear ice water: snow-white exhausted faces, eyes in lifeless darkness. At their backs famine days, unheated rooms, sick infants, gnawing cries of children. It compacted the dark mass of the unemployed, the whole of this open space was now filled with people as tight-packed as if the unmoving tramping stamping people had been truncheoned together, their bodies breathing against each other, twisting and turning against each other, each and every person in that mass was seeking with all their might to escape the weight of other bodies and push their way forward ahead of the others; in this way the mass was constantly thrusting forth and the people pushing in an unceasing slow rolling movement ever harder toward the still-shut factory gates where those who'd arrived first were now only holding themselves upright with great effort and gasping for air, their arms and chests pressed right up against the cold iron of the gates, one of these early arrivers was reaching their arms up the gate, fingers creeping upward and upward, the dark-red terror-struck face already flowed with sweat, eyes foggy and confused as the pressure from behind only increased; the Swede did not know how but he was right in the middle of the sea of people, it closed around him on all sides, heads, shoulders, and a pressure from all around, a weight pressing downward and downward, each body in the mass of bodies wanted to get ahead of the others, above all others; and no one could do a thing, he sensed how it was no longer he himself who was moving, the others were driving him, carrying him, a hot dead moving compulsion. He would never reach the gate by his own might. Between thirty and fifty men it had been said. (But what were all these women doing here, what were they hoping for?)

The factory's clock began to strike. It struck seven strikes. The silence was sick and cold with anticipation. When the final strike had rung out a whining was heard: the gates parted, like a viscid dark river the mass of people began to pour in. But suddenly there was a resistance. Arms and legs began to resist, crowding each other; at once all movement was confused, conflicting. The Swede tried to keep his head up to get air, through the mighty whirl of faces and bodies there was a flash in the factory gates' dark gape – gold, dark, uniforms. A dry smacking sound was heard from that direction, like a sudden pull of air. He couldn't make sense of it. But from the front rows that were now at great speed pushing their way backward over those who were still trying to make their way forward, rose a howl, a terror-struck yelping, it found immediate echo farther away, a few piercing women's screams came first, women who'd already desperately tried to fight their way out, away; but the river of the unemployed kept rushing in from behind, those who were farthest away could distinguish nothing of those in front of them but their napes and backs, they'd understood nothing and tried slowly and inexorably to jostle on. Screams rose to the brightening sky. In a few moments the place was aboil, faces appeared and vanished as if on the crests and troughs of waves; in the distance the row of whirling batons was like a surf break – the first blood-washed faces rocked out into the sea of people like debris from a shipwreck. Rose up, unconscious contorted. Vanished. Vanished.

He sensed that his feet were trampling soft things.

The surf of batons now broke forth, it drove like a wedge through the sea of people. It drew near. He saw a head with bleeding eyes upturned. The air resounded with howls of anguish. Before his gaze something bloody billowed. He felt his knees give out, he didn't have the energy to hold himself up anymore, too heavy was the weight, his temples pounded, it felt as if his chest were being torn to pieces, his gaping mouth cried out without him noticing like an animal facing death. All the while the dead smacking sound plowed its way through the howling mass, ever closer, relentlessly it plowed its furrow of suddenly mute falling bodies straight through those fighting gasping howling. It felt as if something burst inside him – arteries, retina? It went dark. But his limbs continued to fight even in the blood-tinged revolving heat in which he was now tramping, he was tramping as if in a dark fen, as if he were already several meters deep in the dark mud. Then he sensed he was holding someone by the hand.

It was a curious feeling. He was holding a hand, a hand was holding his, it was squeezing his fingers as if it wanted to crush them. Or as if it tugged at him to get him out of the swim of blood in which he was tramping and fighting? In any case he was unable to free himself, someone had attached themselves to him, he was attached to someone.

And it was dark. But he was retrieved from the dark with pains as if he were being birthed. After an endless span of time he found himself again in an alley between rows of dark brick warehouses, suddenly it was silent, he was supporting himself on a wall and vomiting and he watched a bloody sludge spill out. Next he noticed that someone was supporting him, it was a small woman but she looked strong – for some reason he was of the impression that she was not entirely young. Though her face did look quite young, soft and flat: her blank dark eyes stared at him, it was like the stare of an animal. She was bare-headed and tousled and her clothes were ripped and torn at, otherwise she appeared unharmed. And she took his right arm and laid it across her shoulder and as she supported him in this way she took care as she helped him take a seat on the ground. There was a peculiar and strange gentleness in this: and at once he let his head drop heavily to her chest and she held his head in her arms. So they sat.

And so they could have stayed sitting – for all eternity.

For it felt in some way as if this is how everything should be – for all eternity. This was the correct state of things: it was simple. Warmth: the warmth of this other body. Silence, the aliveness via the other's beating heart. It wasn't more complicated than this, one needn't look farther, this was how everything should be.

But eternity was not here, not now. They had to start saying words to each other, hard to reach heavy words, time-tattered, coarsened by others' fumbling, the stuttering, the searching around in the silence that should not be broken (like the searching of fingertips and lips across a still-obscure body, at the shoreline the pale living heat). So they found themselves walking along the dark blind brick walls: speaking words. But they could not bring themselves to part. And he went with her to her room, it was a room with a bed at the top of a dirty building near St. Mark's Place: what were they to say to each other? in haste an achingly raw embrace transpired. Then the Swede's powers were drained and he sank back down into a painful flickering half-slumber, so lay he for two days: the crush had been dire.

The woman he'd ended up with was Polish by birth. In the room with the bed where he lay (where the first night he woke screaming that something was touching him, soft, hot, strange, an entire strange body was breathing beside him, touching the full length of his body) was a wood-burning heater and a table with a portable stove and a basin; under the bed was a suitcase where under her dirty nightgown she kept a rosary made of small black wooden beads, a worn prayer card of Our Lady of Częstochowa slick with grease and a blurry brown group photo depicting a lively family, there were at least thirty people who'd posed for the traveling photographer's box camera in the small village in eastern Poland some time before the outbreak of the world war. They were now all dead.

(All dead: little brother little sister, she'd combed her hair with a comb made of bone, a filthy silk bow drooping in her long hair, they were dead, all were dead, they beat like waves against distant walls, the dark hidden place of pilgrimage washed over by sea and waves Lord grant unto them eternal rest may the eternal Light shine upon them Only she remained she'd lost them and could not find her way home through waves, darkness, time)

shine upon them

But she was so alone.

Living here in bed and out of suitcase. And there were times when she'd managed to keep herself afloat. Other times were mostly like a dark hole, a downward spiral – but it had come to an end, had she been brought to the surface again: how? Mostly a dishwasher, a bottle rinser at the brewery. But everything always went wrong, it was as if she couldn't bring about anything lasting in the external world, was forever being left behind like something spent, used – her body was being used up used but her face bore no trace of this, it stayed as soft and flat and unmarked with dark blank newborn eyes. But she wasn't particularly young. And her room was a room that remembered much confusion of the cold-sweating unnameable kind. (And it was in this bed that she'd once lain with the probe inside her and the torments began and made their way through her as dark red terrible billows and she mumbled without pause, almost beyond consciousness, how did they bring me – o God o God how did they bring me to this?) But on the third day when the Swede woke up and propped himself up on his elbow in the bed and the sun was high; and through the window that faced roofs and smoke the spring light broke in like a wall, the bed, the table, the walls shone and flowed with sun and the woman sat by the window, small dark and heavy with light around her limbs; he felt in that moment that he had come home.

And they lay in the red dusk in complete silence. Their bodies had spoken. Their limbs had spoken. But incomprehensibly. Inaccessibly.

And they couldn't imagine parting. They lay silent in the red and knitted their fingers together, tight. So he went on living there.

Thus passed the spring. There was no work to be had. The season helped somewhat, it came and warmed the starved bodies heavy with cold. The lime trees burst into filthy leaf. But in the Swede's mind unemployment was beginning to leave its mark – scarlike furrows took shape, deep, ingrained. For what was difficult was not only the absence of food and everything else right when he wanted to make a home with the woman he'd found. What was truly difficult and couldn't be overwon was that life had cast him back: unfit! – out into the darkness from whence he came. Found to be superfluous. So it was. The Polish woman caressed him like a child, she wished with all her might for a child. But there was no work to be had. And misfortune grew with each passing day, ever more impossible to chase away, it swelled and darkened, they were sliding toward the ocean. Spring's smudged gray-warm twilight bathed these resigned bodies, these rugged faces. Still there was life. But not much hope. There was no child. But they clung to each other like children in a dark curious sibling-bed. New York had become a sea, the uncertain ocean of hunger and death.

The raiment of her memories was stiff with dirt and secretions: this fell from her body. This belonged to a dead body; this did not belong to the real and living one; and this fell from her like rags, straw. He was her first. Everything else belonged to her alone – her costumed self: the wild lack of strength, the tugging in her limbs, the indifferent bodies breaking their way in. They prised and broke and remained alien. He was her first. And she carried him within, wherever she looked within herself there he was.

This was her first time. Beyond him she was dead. Beyond his body, her body was shadow, disease, moldering.

And she saw before her a child of him: the child's face. But nothing came of it, perhaps it was the half-starvation. Months passed and her womb remained empty.

And the closer he was to her, the more distant he seemed: the nearer, the more he closed himself off. They slept, they shared what there was to eat, undressed, dressed. But someone in him did not want to be captured. Someone in him was on the run. Didn't want to. Was already far away. The nights grew hot and difficult toward the summer in the room right below the roof: below them in the smoky night mist the massive city mumbled and roared (like a great animal moves in its sleep with silvery sweat-gleaming limbs in the heat-hazed dusk); the Polish woman had trouble sleeping and in half-wakefulness she was hunted by something, something evil was drawing near, rising up like pincers out of what was dark and gleaming and resembled a sea; and in the hot stifling darkness she began to cry, she lay herself upon the Swede's body and kissed his proud white chest and heavy shoulders and the tears flowed bitterly across her mouth. But he did not wake up: he was sleeping like a tree, strange, unreachable, without shame and mercilessly like a tree, a clawed animal keeps guard in the tree even after its branches have come crashing to the ground, the crown become a lair of ash: a great animal of death roves freely in the silent aftermath, howling in the flames – eyes shining, muscles at play under skin shimmering with its finally won (or re-won) freedom.

She sensed that the animal was beginning to make its way out again, it had never been tamed, it had simply laid down and slept a while deep inside. The animal looked at her through his eyes with its peculiar extinguished gaze. It sat in there behind his eyes, it was in the process of digging itself out into his features: a rough tiger face, a lion's muzzle hungering for death. The animal paws embraced her.

The Polish woman went to church, lit a candle for Our Lady of Częstochowa. The mother of the sea of people looked upon her.

But one day early in the summer the Swede vanished. He stayed away a day or two, then he was back, no explanation. And for a while after that he was gone again and then he didn't come back, not that day, not the next – he did not come back. He was gone.

The Polish woman went to church and lit a candle.

And she saw before her a dark sea: shoreless. At the world's end. And there no human voice could be heard anymore, only the sighing, lamenting winds – restless, restless.

The winds lamented. The souls lamented.

Holy shadowless light why have you left us? Holy One, where do you lay dead?

The Polish woman clung to the room they'd lived in as if for dear life, as to a shipwreck in high seas – she could not surrender it, the room was the last tie, without it he'd never be able to find her again when he returned. There was no work to be had. She washed dishes here and there, and so was sometimes given a meal. But the rent was always due and rent had to be paid, she could not surrender the room, if she did he'd never find her again. So for a time and in emergency she sold her body, it was only when it regarded the rent that she went that way, never to procure something for herself, something to eat for example – she'd rather starve to death, this she knew. The room was a different matter and greater than food, it had to be saved at any cost. And she managed to hold on to it. But autumn came and with it the cold: she felt that she was close to giving up. She roamed the docks. The water was enticing, it was dark, cold, empty. It was enticing. But then the owner of a little bar called to her: as in a fog she walked into the bar, it was crowded and dirty: the bar owner poured a glass of rum for her and told her to drink – he'd seen enough, he said, whatever her situation, a drink would help. She gave him a muddled look: what did he want in return? – but he wanted nothing in return, he simply wanted to give her a drink because he'd seen her roaming around out there (confused, confused: how could everything have come to this?) and he thought it looked like she needed a drop of something strong. That's all there was to it. And she drank; and she did not go into the water. And when she was back in her room (it was already dark) the Swede had returned: he was rolled up in her blanket on the floor (she'd had to part with the bed). He looked up at her with a bewildered extinguished dead gaze. Without a word he reached out his arms for her.

(Well, he'd been swindled. Thoroughly swindled. And now it really was over – all of it.

At last he'd arrived at a town that lay in the middle of the desert. He'd hiked a long time to get there, not a cent left for the bus, moreover no one in Los Alamos – where a barkeeper talked and talked all night about all the opportunities, brilliant, dazzling, undiscovered, unexploited that were to be found in a desert town – seemed to know from where and when a bus might be running or if there even was one. From a distance it had resembled a heap of dry dung eaten out and burrowed through by larvae and beetles that had now left it so all that remained was a labyrinth of collapsed passageways and paths like the miles-wide dried-out riverbed barely visible on the blinding hot ash-white plain. The town was made up of barracks in lines straight as arrows. In the wide far too wide streets that lay like deserted fields between the half-collapsed and abandoned rows of barracks corroded by the sun, silence stood seething hot, leaden, mighty. It was as if someone were standing there: made of lead, palpable. Once at a sort of town square, a great open space where the dust whirled up in pillars of cloud, blinding ash-white cloud columns, were proper buildings as far as buildings went in these parts: a type of hut of chalky mud with curtains made of wooden beads at the entrance. The silence was the same: stifling, burning, a body in fever. But outside one of the houses a white mule was hitched, along its walls sat some Indians with their hats pulled down over their faces, legs outstretched. One of them was old, staring unblinking out into the white lead-heat: he was blind – instead of a gaze his eyes were a crawling star-flickering mass. The Indians by the white chalk wall – part of the wall covered by windworn scraps of posters – were like shadows, beneath the brims of their hats theirs faces became pits of darkness, a well, deep within was the glimpse of a dead water, extinguished water across cold dark stones. He'd been swindled. The barkeeper in Los Alamos now spent his nights talking about how he'd managed to lure a poor fool to a desert town that for twenty years had been empty of all human life but for the shadowlike Indians, a town like the half-annihilated remnants of a termite mound. His knees quaked. He'd arrived at the end, he felt it as clearly as if he'd touched it, the burning dense lifeless body of silence: he was at the end. He fumbled in the light, the square with the buildings, the Indians, the sight of the mule through a quaking clear veil of heat, soaring, burning like endlessly slow-falling ash. With outstretched hands he approached a wall: a building wall. Searching all along it, staggering, fumbling as if at dusk but in the full glare of the sun. He sat on the ground, leaned his back against the hot clay wall, pulled his hat over his eyes, and so he took his place among the shadows.)

(He returned. Gingerly, he carried his strange burning heavy head.

He walked around at midday on a street on the east side aswarm with people, high above the street the rustling net of metal cables, then the silence returned, somewhere from within him it rose up, soundless, dense, building walls, faces, cables, an elevated railway in the air of bows and nets above the roofs and floating letters from advertisements turned clear, quaking as if seen through a veil of slowly falling white ash. And he fumbled as if he had no eyes, he staggered through the middle of the day as if it were dusk.

Then he remembered the room. And returned there.)

His shimmering dead eyes. Damaged, that was her sense of him.

And she received him in her arms like a child, a stranger and a guest, mute like dark fishes they play in the depths, slippery bodies gliding through the depths, through one another, limbs speaking to each other in the language of darkness, nocturnal words between bodies expressed.

At this time it often happened that the unemployed who were not American citizens were deported, that is to say their residence permit was not renewed, when it expired the American government would give them a one-way ticket back to where they came from. The winter of '29–'30 was the most difficult. Come spring it seemed to ease a bit. But then the summer arrived, the dead period. Moreover August 1930 was very hot. On the 15th of August in the evening a conflagration erupted at St. Mark's Place, a child on the third floor had been playing with matches, the building was quickly engulfed and the conflagration spread like a blast to the nearby properties, it was to be the largest neighborhood fire in the history of New York. Claimed by the fire was Viktor Lindgren from Bäck in Ljungby in Sweden, his Polish-born wife (they'd married some months before) was saved. But she had lost her papers, work permit, and residence permit and the authorities did not see cause to issue a fresh set, for far too long had she been in want of steady work, she was referred to the consulate where the marriage had been registered, there she could obtain a new marriage certificate: the American authorities decided that she (at the expense of the American government) be repatriated to the country that she via her late husband had citizenship. And two months after the Swede was killed in the fire she was standing on the deck of the Swedish American Line's *Gripsholm*, watching New York drift away, en route to the address the consulate had procured and that she had written on a piece of paper fixed with a safety pin to her coat or rather her overcoat's inner pocket (she'd been dressed by a charitable organization): Judit and Albert Lindgren, *Bäck pa Ljungby, Sweden.* Two months on she was still absent, emptied of all, this alone with its fearsome arbitrary strength was alive inside her: how the man she'd lived with sank down – one moment earlier he'd been there, reeling with sooted face in the midst of flame, mad-eyed, hair and clothes in flames, etched by fire, bright with fire was the bed, the table, the pots, and the portable stove (they'd managed to cobble together many such a thing ahead of their marriage), these things were lifted up in the shining white fireglow – a moment of never before sensed splendor, consuming gemstone splendor before it collapsed into bright embers then an ash resolved of impure fragments, smelt, cracked enamel, clumps of metal, smoke-browned porcelain shards, gray ash, black ash, death-black sticky ash, death-black sticky something the great horrific object under the tarp down on the street where the air was as hot as an oven, dark gray the stifling dawning all the while sped and flashed through with a smarting rain of sparks, all the while things exploded inside the caved-in smoking neighborhood sending wisps and scours of sparks into the heavy gray that was a hot cloth upon the face, the chest where the heart was pounding as if the world were only made up of mad pulsing gushes of blood – between each beat was a silence hollow as the silence in a burned-out echoing stairwell; an unconsciousness, a bottomless hole and the chest right up against a burning wall, impossible to move away from, impossible to breathe, sips of air with burning gum, lips searing off; yonder the flames stand seven stories high, fifteen stories high, the iron bridge sways amidst the moving roaring mountain of fire, deep with fire, iron girders soften give way viscid and slow as rubber, draping slowly from their stays, collapsing with loosed chunks of facade in a cloud of glowing limedust down into the flaming abyss; it burns tall as mountains, deep as sea, white, a feast of death, something lies beneath the tarpaulin, something large that seems to be flowing apart, running thick as tar and as endlessly heavy, heavier than lead: *that*, the man she'd been living with (the police told her as much, but she wasn't allowed to lift the tarp, they dragged her away, only a corner did she manage to tug up). Between them flamed the flames sky high, storm high – between her and *that*. And the silence of the fire that at once as if in a single violent soundless detonation drowned out all the world-city's sounds. The foghorns boomed in the fire fog down by the river, deep down they bellowed and roared like wounded animals, but the silence broke in as if the whole world were exploding, ear drums, windowpanes, shafts of bone burst and turned to dust under this enormous pressure. And it was truly silent; perfectly silent. From the soft asphalt one could have collected buckets of fried sparrows and pigeons had one so wished. And the white sea flamed, flamed: fire! death – by – fire!

And so there came one day a letter from the State Department about a death in America, Viktor Gustaf Lindgren born in Bäck, Ljungby, Kristianstad County, the second of April 1893, died in New York the fifteenth of August 1930. Destitute. Survived by widow.

Judit walked into the potato fields with the letter.

"Viktor is dead," she said with no particular expression at all.

Thereupon she looked down at the letter and read with questioning tone:

"Survived by widow – ?"

Albert took off his hat, for something must be done when a death is announced. Unreality, absence fixed itself to the moment like the silent clinging white fog that on this morning stickily crept across haulm and furrow. "So Viktor married – " he muttered, mostly to say something. Judit's eyes seemed to have sunk into her head; deep inside they lay clear and ghastly in their dark hollows.

One year before (a day identical to the day of the death announcement, in white fog, with wafts of wet clay earth and haulm, with wafts of wrack and sea) the same thing happened to Albert that happened to his father Johan Lindgren that time he walked across the heath to Torp.

And he fell upon his face among the clay mounds in worship.

Thereafter life seemed to be so short, but a moment, the moment was almost over, time was near its end. Still it was day. But night had almost caught up with the white autumn day (the scents in the fog). Soon the thin milky membrane of light would burst. And night take its place. Endmost and ultimate.

And cast in a light like ash; a death light – their faces: petrifactions.

And he lay face down in the field in worship.

After that he went home. But the farm and the house and the things and the day, its damp smell of haulm, and the night, its dark sea-susurrus, was as usual – the master of life had shown itself and life had shown itself to be as it was, not different, curious but not different, it was not for the sake of redemption that he'd had to lie face down in worship but so that he might live, to be pushed into the ground and covered with earth and darkness like a seed of life.

But Albert had very much wanted to be delivered and also taken up.

Albert was afraid of death. His fear of death was a secret he was unable to conceal from himself, all too often it burst forth, rushing in like autumn water over flat helpless meadows. Far too often. And he had never touched a woman, this had not come to pass.

Albert was afraid of death. And he had never touched a woman.

With time he had become a large heavy man that mostly appeared lifelessly gray-white – he whitened outward, whitened outward from the nose from within the dark-colored corners of his eyes, became white of nose and fingertip, had colorless lips that tended to blue, cold hands and feet. He was frozen, stubborn and slow in his way. Had very sweaty feet. Like his father he had a big prematurely grizzled brown beard. His back-combed dark hair had now also begun to gray. He had an irresistible need to always have clean freshly laundered underwear closest to his body; Judit saw to it that he had access to stain-free white shirts, one for each day, and clean undergarments. The white of the shirt, the ever-unsoiled neckband, the invariable smell of freshly laundered linen and foot sweat was particular to him, the smell he was known by. The whiteness, as far as outward appearances go, distinguished him from others, otherwise he walked around like everyday people did in general, in old worn-out clothing: a pair of trousers of a now indeterminable shade, darned woolen sweaters and on Sunday like everyday a green slipover that couldn't be called particularly clean, this tormenting desire for cleanliness applied only to what was closest to his body, the desire for cleanliness that in fact resembled rock-hard unbending grinding lust.

He had very much wanted to at once be delivered and taken up, it was so difficult, all of it – difficult from the start, too heavy, time made nothing less heavy and pressing and complicated, the years settled in his limbs like an impurity, depositing in his heart a sediment that defiled his every thought, it was heavy and impure, thus he had headaches, all the while he might also burst into fits of tears – no different to when he was a child, in the middle of the field, just like that, for no apparent reason. The shifting delicate gaze. It was so difficult, all of it, moving from day to day, just going on and on through all the heaviness, alone, a clinging stickiness.

He had very much wanted in one fell swoop to be delivered. From the earth.

He'd never touched a woman, this had been his secret shame. However now he was reading the Scriptures, again and again he read a passage he'd been pondering for some time. And one day he found that he could truly count himself among the one hundred and forty-four thousand who follow the Lamb whithersoever he goeth, they doeth so already here on earth, they are already in paradise. He had an unsettled inkling around this, it was as if he'd twisted and distorted the vision somewhat – but had he not earned his place in paradise, in all these years he had of course never defiled himself with women. But in this he sensed an inkling of untruthfulness. And perchance to drive away this inkling he came to comport himself in a slightly peculiar manner, he the taciturn one who'd never been able to get more than two or three words out in a row, he talked about this wherever he went: he turned to the clergy, among them he delighted in joyful siblinghood, or near-siblinghood, he still did not belong to the community but he had begun to pay regular visits to the mission hall, his conversion was anticipated; and there was pious sighing in pious cottages over brother Albert's virginity. But he sensed an inkling of untruthfulness. And he couldn't help but expound on it, not just with the congregants but with everyone he met, suddenly he was traveling around the region, in all type of farm, pious and impious, he made his eccentricity known.

But he did sense an inkling of untruthfulness. And as God does not allow himself to be mocked, his punishment did come. For when his effusive expounding upon this great wonder did not end, a hint of a hint of a furtive sneer came into the listener's mien, the sighs came to bear notable resemblance to muffled chuckling, even among the congregants these smiles spread. Soon there was open laughter across the entire region. There may be miracles, it was said, in which mother nature herself played a part. Albert caught on in the end: the day arrived when it was crystal clear to him – then the world was turned on its head and broke apart, he hid like a horror-struck child high up in the attic where it was most dark, in vain Judit stood at the attic stairs, calling out that he had to get some food into him, but he would not respond anymore, it was like when he was a child. The next morning he emerged dusty and floury and full of cobwebs; his eyes wild, red from weeping. After that he never went back to the mission hall; and only reluctantly into his own village. He worked the field and, in the barn, he ate and slept heartily. He often had headaches. He was as he was, change he did not. And he understood that whether he was pure or impure, it had nothing to do with God. God was above all such as it was now, above the living and the dead.

And the Lord had brought about his fall and he was once more a poor sullied longer like all the rest.

And with that Albert stopped lying, as best he could nary an untrue word passed his lips, nor through his heart. But neither did any other word for that matter, he barely dared move anymore, all went mute outside as well as in, how could he dare speak up again?

But he read the Scriptures; like his father had, he would take down the Scriptures each night from the shelf above the kitchen table, he read and followed the words with his index finger, this was his comfort, in this way he offered his every longing up to God's mercy and thus hoped for redemption. With time he became notably versed in the Good Book.

But he never did go out, years passed without him even at a distance seeing any woman other than his sister. But right through this serious longing, this heaviness and impurity and emptiness he persisted with hope, God would not betray him, he told himself.

But wrecks they sink into the depths of mud:

in the depths darkness without day the human without faith sinks too, all of a human that is not faith, like an ancient ship stripped of mast, oar, rudder, she is driven across unruly waters, the currents carrying her deteriorating body across the depths, the currents dragging her down into darkening whirls, down below where dense schools of eel crowd in the current of black water, the mud sucks, seagrass the color of death, thus death sucks her faith down into the darkening whirls.

Lord have mercy on us, from a mother's womb from a mother's teat come the serfs of death, wearing our faces like masks drawn upon gliding decay, like the water-white paint of the figurehead flakes upon the rotting spongy wood of the sinking ship, sucked into the whirls, sinking – Lord have mercy!

And once several years ago the Queen had one day walked a path of trepidation, a path of unreasonable expectation across the heath to Torp. Perhaps a year had passed since she'd seen the little girl, Victor's offspring, in the store. One year – no, more for she'd seen her in early spring, a still-snowy March day (the snowpack was heavy, close to a thaw when the old woman set off with her load and the little one atop her load toward the forest and the heath). And now it was autumn, the second autumn since that encounter and Viktor had been in the States for a year, they'd had a single letter informing them that he'd arrived, all was well and he was looking confidently into the future. And now it was autumn, such had time run away. And the girl she'd seen came to her at night in dreams; she was playing with a ball, then she came over so the Queen would play with her, came to her lap to be caressed, wrapped her arms tightly around the Queen's neck. Again and again the child came to her in dreams. In this way her dreams at night became what was in fact real, daytime was but empty.

On a clear beautiful autumn day she crossed the heath. The forest rose blue above the heath. It was so quiet in the still sunshine, the moss and twigs gleamed red, the migratory birds had gone their way. It was time to harvest the sloe. Down there the sea shone blue and placid. In her bundle was a dress that she'd sewn. She wondered if the little one might find her a bit rough on the eyes, hands too great and hard, by the look of her it had always been apparent that her way with things was too tough and hard – might she feel afraid of her?

She was more afraid than she'd ever been before as she walked in the calm golden clear autumn light – one could see for miles all around, down by the road the birch trees burned yellow, each leaf distinct and shining, down there in the birches swarmed the mourning cloaks (a soundless dark flutter across her field of vision then gone, one can almost not claim to have seen them), the final messengers. All else silent and gone. She'd sewn a dress but now she could clearly see how clumsy the seams were, she never did have the time and energy to practice this finer type of work. And her steps drove her relentlessly on, there was nothing to do about it, she was almost there.

In Torp the old woman, the maternal grandmother, received the dress with stiff hands. And set it aside. Through the window the Queen saw a dark-haired child, a girl, playing at a distance, over by the chicken hutch, and could not quite discern the girl's features – could not see what she'd become; could not see how she was at all. And clearly no one intended to summon her. It was clear that they did in no way intend to. The mother of the girl had now also arrived: she was ever young, straight-backed and strong. She had a beautiful face. They had beautiful faces, the folks over in Torp: beautiful, strong, peculiar. And they were unyielding. It was with them that the girl had her home. Nowhere else. No question.

The Queen found herself bent over the table with her face in her hands. If only she could cry. But there was only emptiness, death. She couldn't imagine ever being able to stand back up, to go. She sat like that with her face in her hands, slumped. Someone touched her; it was the old woman. Well, she should go. It was time for her to go. And this was the end.

She walked out blindly. Over by the chicken hutch the dark-haired child played. She did not look up, she carried on carefree; she was playing with stones, tossing them ahead of her.

Later, through the years, she'd catch sight of the little girl. Her braids down to her waist, glossy dark. Her appearance as fine and hard as glass. And her shining eyes caught the light in a sudden great flash, fire. She was said to be implacable, uncommonly headstrong.

Thus passed the winters. Washing the supper dishes, Judit's gaze was large empty dead – dark, empty, strange like the wide dark night just outside the kitchen window. Her hands were busy – washing dishes, rinsing, drying. Mending, mending. But Viktor was away and remained so. And night was upon them, its briny roar, barely a kilometer below the Baltic gushed icy black across the pebbled beach, it sounds so close.

And with this they knew he was dead.

But as if that weren't enough shortly thereafter another letter arrived, this time from the consulate in New York. Informing them that his widow was on her way. What?

Well, yes, his widow was on her way.

That day Judit and Albert could only stare at each other over supper.

And the Queen went to the chairman of the municipal council, this was the closest official she could think of (since the village constable was more of an underling, a henchman). She showed him the letter with the consulate's stamp. He scratched his head: what in tarnation?

But the widow was on her way.

Wasn't this the most natural course of action, he wondered shyly. After all a sibling would be her closest relation. Besides Victor's widow did hold a share in the farm.

But to the Queen nothing about this was natural. But what was there to do? – this stranger was already on her way.

She thought he was looking at her with a curious and equivocal smile.

Then it struck her like a blow: the farm! If she asks to take out her share. The farm won't hold.

And she closed herself off, her face went white and tense, she bade a quick farewell. She thought: I knew enemies were all around. Now it's confirmed. Now I am certain.

At night Judit dreamed that she was awake. She heard a knock at the door – not at the kitchen entrance but at the great front door, the one that bride and groom first encounter as they walk in and the door through which the dead are carried out. And from where she lay on the kitchen settle she watched herself rise and cross the floor to the table and pull out the drawer where the candles were kept (the electrical wiring was shoddy, there were frequent shorts) and light a candle and walk across the floor, protecting the flame with her hand as she unlocked the door to the entryway. The night wind tore through the treetops, the alders bending to skim the ground by the brook, their pained creaking as they straightened back up, could be heard all the way up here: louder than all else was the surge of the sea. The apple tree's branches scraped the entryway's windows. For a moment the woman with the candle stood perfectly still before the great front door. Then came more knocking. The woman undid the bolt, the light gave a violent flicker, the door opened onto a wall of gusting wet darkness. But no human being was to be seen, only rain and darkness and the billowing contorting shapes of trees in the night. The women cupped her hand around the flame and spied into the dark. Under those wide eyelids her eyes in candlelight were like great transparent marbles – glass marbles filled with water mirroring flames a thousandfold like a reception hall with dark mirrors reflecting mirror and flame, flame and mirror, into infinity.

Next the light shifted, she looked like a swollen animal. A hunkering blackish sodden being vanished across the threshold into the darkness.

Hour after hour passed over her on the kitchen settle. The wind tore through the darkness outside, the sea roared. It was as if her whole life were careening and coming about keel to the wind, now here it came driven blindly, a dead empty hull in the waves across dead gray-shining slabs.

From the depths. From the depths.

This is how it came to be that in the autumn of 1930, during the depression, rumors began to go around Ljungby parish that the Queen in Bäck and her virgin brother Albert were expecting a guest from America.

And indeed one day said guest arrived – in curious fashion for the village constable arrived with her in a taxi cab, in the middle of the night she'd knocked wet and muddy in that long cumbersome sopping overcoat on the door of a farm far at the other end of the parish, the folks there understood neither her words nor her gestures or her odd alien vagrantlike beggarly guise, they let her sleep in the hay loft but sealed the house tight around them and the next morning the second it was possible they sent for the village constable the one who'd revealed himself to have been kept abreast of the situation, he'd known a widow was to be expected; then it came to pass that the deceased Viktor Lindgren's widow made her entry into Bäck with police escort and in a taxi cab and at the expense of the county council. She did not look like people did in Ljungby (even if there were Galician workers several dozen miles away up in Bromölla). She was muddy – dried mud – up past her ankles. She looked peculiar, the very half-drifting half-filthy sort of person for whom the father had opened the door, that he practically sought out so that in the end it was uncertain what was true goodness and what was no more than something dissolved, moldering inside him that turned toward what was familiar, downward, downward to the permissive, compelling, free. The Queen now looked upon her adversary, standing there gripping her small worn bag stuffed full (one could only imagine the tat it contained, rags and broken bits of the kind a child stubbornly saves and regards as a treasure trove). The adversary was now in the house and had come to stay. The adversary was skin to skin now, now it was a question of whether or not they had it in them to resist, whirling and sucking down there at their feet was the whole grey, oozing, dissolving sea of poverty, once a foot slips in you're done for, in less than a blink of the eye it will have sucked you down and sucked the clothes from your body, the flesh from your bones, your face from your empty skull, it was a matter of watching yourself, it was a matter of not giving in. The adversary stood with its bag wearing its curiously fashioned coat which was without a doubt a refashioned man's overcoat, in that needful hazy uncertain face her eyes were like an animal's. Never reveal your need, thought the Queen. Above all, never this. If you reveal your need you're doomed. It relegates you to those down there. Those on the other side. The widow standing here with her bag belonged down there by garment and body and even by smell, a cloying unwashed stench of poverty, the smell of the other side, clung to her. So at last the adversary had made its way here, all the way in, was standing there in the kitchen with her pitiful overcoat and bag, all the while the village constable governed and orated. I won't give in, thought the Queen. Never give in. And her father's face appeared before her. Never give up, she said to the dead man's face, it was strange, care-worn, full of peace. I do not want his peace, not as such, I will not give in. And she grabbed the foreigner's arm hard and shoved her in the direction of the door, in this manner she led her across the farm to the barn, there was a room on the north side that had previously served as a tack room and tool shed and catch-all, a fire couldn't be lit in there but it was warmed somewhat by the wall it shared with the cows, warmth could always be found with them, here the woman would now live – it was not because the Queen was cruel, she simply did not want this woman in the house, how was one to sleep peacefully at night?

(but sleep was a struggle in any case, it was as if through the walls and masonry and right across the farm the Queen could hear the strange breaths, the strange movements, it is as if she could *see* her right through the walls and darkness – the Queen lurches from sleep, she does *see* her in the darkness: her gray body with her heavy abdomen and hips on the mattress under the blankets, that sleeping frightening childlike face)

A crown of hay for the Queen. A crown of death. Thus the gray-white stone face, death-crowned. Eyes clear pits of death, death flames cast fire-shadows through the clear globes of the eyes, fire-shadows across dead shimmering damp skin, across bone, wax, sick.

And Viktor's widow

her eyes were flush with her skin as so often with infants, dark, blank, not moving much, the gaze of one who has been pushed and shoved around blind alleys too often to even be able to comprehend any longer

(dark as caves serpentine slick glittering with anxious intestine wetness)

and all the gaze understands is this: it can't be true. *Cannot* be true! Hence she'd acquired that dark gleaming empty gaze, gleaming hollow as if the globes of the eyes had been dug out but the emptied pit was still covered by a glossy membrane or bubble about to burst into empty wetness.

So now the widow was eating the Queen's bread, but the Queen made her work for this food. It's matter of defending yourself when the rats come out of the rotting flood plains, from the stench of stagnant waterlogged fields. She smelled of tinker, the Polish woman did.

But she was strong, and she could carry water and sacks of potato, she picked up the saw. And upon finishing one task she'd look expectantly at Judit and a nervous tense smile would fly across that smooth face. But the Queen did not smile back. And the Polish woman's smile went dark, her face became empty and impoverished again. After a while she stopped smiling at all, she simply looked empty and sluggish, sometimes the Queen had to give her a shove to get her to understand.

So the Queen had acquired another weakling over whom to command. And command she did. The Polish woman wasn't allowed to show herself outside of the farm, far less was she entrusted with errands to the store; so it came to be that very few had seen her, folks eventually began to joke that Judit must be keeping her tethered to the sheep pen – time passed, winter passed, it was spring and still barely a soul had laid eyes on Viktor's widow, the farm in Bäck had swallowed her up, now someone was claiming to *know* that if you walked up to the wall of the Lindgren siblings' barn there'd be movement and moaning like an animal's sighs but with human voice. But truth be told not much more of Albert was seen either, one saw him at a distance working far out in a field but if folks started in his direction he'd abandon plow and horse and dash off – when he sometimes couldn't avoid meeting someone on the village road, he said, as was now to be expected, nothing at all, he fingered his clean white shirt and his gaze was as shifting as ever, it was as if he weren't quite alive.

It was such that Albert's sense of self had once been wounded. It could not be forgotten, it was as if that moment had rendered him unfit for being human, he could no longer be among people like others could, he had gone lame and so he dragged himself and his lame lower body across ground and rock, he stayed this way, he did not get to where he was going.

(the memory could appear at any moment, as with a burning glass: the man in Hulta farm – there it had taken place – who flung himself upon the table bawling with laughter: oh Albert, oh Albert – !)

And it was in this way that his self had come to harm. It was no longer fit for use, that's how it felt, what was human-real in him was gone, as if it had never been. All gone, inaccessible –

– with a single cut, a human reality moved far far away. And he didn't dare venture beyond the village, he could sense how choking laughter snuck after him, at his back behind: fingers at his back. It was like an all-encompassing white almost blinding haze. Town lay beyond: that hole of darkness full of people, eyes, fingers, there one was dragged in and stripped naked before them all, full of eyes and fingers, there one stood naked, white, ugly and all were looking on. It was evil. And he stayed in the white haze, things and animals surrounded by radiant haze, above all else he loved the silence in the white haze upon the water as he drew up his net, all that could be heard was the beating of his own heart, the water, the water dripping from the oar, the fish gleaming in the boat. The white fog, the whitish gray silent water, the water-glossed dark rocky shore. One morning when he was rowing landward a cow was standing out in the water between the rocks, large, still, brown, steaming she stood there in the water, ruminating and looking at him – he then saw that her large hot body was as if wreathed with rays and even her eyes were fringed with rays but rays the color of blood. It steamed hotly from her damp-darkened loins. He rested his oars and watched her standing there, still, steaming, radiant, God's creature.

But now a new female being had arrived at the farm, as good as mute, true, no better in conversation than cows and their calves, true – but he wasn't much more talkative himself. Albert went around there, looking. His brother's widow seemed to him uncommonly pleasing to the eye, but this did not cause him to be overly friendly or outwardly pleasant, he followed Judit's warning to not give an inch for one cannot know where an inch may lead. But he walked around there, looking: she walked around there, small, gray, extinguished and carried water buckets. Eyes like an animal's.

And he thought one day: Perchance this is the sign. God, my God would not betray me.

Thus passed the time.

And one day it was as if a wave were washing through him, a great cleansing swell of heat, never had he felt anything like it, it seemed to dislodge everything: never, never in his life had he felt such compassion for any being as for this mute wretch of the female sex who here walked.

After this everything was changed. It wasn't unmoving anymore. He was no longer lame. Everything could happen.

She'd come across the Atlantic. She was a plundered vessel: shadows, empty fireshadows solely. She remembered nothing. But her lurching womb sought the dead man. This she carried with her, inside her, this wish to have his child. She walked in her dream, she followed the dead man's tracks – from the kitchen entryway to the barn, from barn to field, in the aftermath this is how she lived her own life with him, he was always inside her, he rested there in silence but alive, it was as if she were carrying him unborn inside her, his heat was there and his vital weight, she chatted with him, he held his tongue but the heat in her responded, so it was as if she were with child, as if she were carrying one of the living.

The Queen walked unmoving, said not one unnecessary word to anyone; commanded; then held her tongue. She'd had a memorial stone raised in the Ljungby cemetery – his name could not be put on the parents' gravestone because of course his ashes were not at rest there but elsewhere, in the States' strange earth, perhaps on a pile of refuse, the Queen dreamed, she had dreams of great trash dumps, immense landscapes of waste, ash, rats. She had raised a memorial of polished granite:

Viktor Gustaf Lindgren
born 2 April 1893 in Bäck † 15 August 1930
in New York USA
I am afloat on a roaring sea
On the true beach of joy.
Sw. Ps. 555

She visited it often. Then she'd sit a long while on the iron bench that stood between the parents' graves and the stone for Viktor. She looked out over the naked gray country. In the far distance was the gray sea. Winter clouds flew forth.

Thus passed the time.

And a year passed.

And then came the day when Albert saw the Polish woman, carefully as a cat, push open the door to the north chamber, the chamber with the gold wallpaper where his father had died – she looked around, this was clearly a habit of hers, then she slunk in. Albert was in his stocking feet and followed her soundlessly in. Then through the crack of the door he watched her standing there, following with her finger the gold flowers' wonderful tendrils across the mute black background. He pushed open the door and stepped in. She stiffened, with unmoving blank eyes like a rabbit without a chance to flee into its burrow. He went right up to her and she did not move, she was paralyzed with fear. Through the chamber window the doleful leafless alders could be seen, down the slope hidden under the frost-seared cow parsley and blackening wild cumin ran the roily brook foaming with the leafy autumn rainwater, decaying plant parts, tangled nests of brown rush, then he grabbed her by the arms. After, he let her go. After, he took her right hand, it was small, red, hard and chapped, and slowly straightened her fingers out one by one, he looked at her hand its fingers, alive and worn with cracked nails, he saw this and felt it to be a great wonder, such hot dry humanity in the flesh, he felt his head whirl and dim, and with this he let go of her hand.

And though this mostly happens at night, the kingdom of night does at times break into the shrieking white daylight so that a human Who-Intends-To, a human Able-and-Willing simply disappears. Like a mantle split. Suddenly there you are, changed. (A few hours later the mantle is whole, sealed, thick, unslit as if nothing had come to pass, the change is barely even a memory, no more than a worrying induration in the mind, some distant stinging – something – something –)

And somewhere in the midst of the white haze he finds himself in the act of prising open a hot living sex, he is someone who cries and who caresses strange hot limbs, and they move and respond (albeit in a distant weak way as if they were searching for something in a dream, something far away, something that lost its way, lost itself), he was crying and caressing, and she too was in motion and mumbling endearments. But it was in another language and to someone else. She was moving and caressing in a dream. The person she was touching and caressing was not there. He was covered by the tarpaulin. And she was touching him in a dream.

And the person he was embracing was no longer human.

That had ended in the flames.

And was consumed. By the flames. The flames.

And nothing real existed. The flames that once were existed. And they flamed inside her, empty. She could not be reached.

And suddenly in the midst of tears and surging waves he understood that something in the human being underneath him was deeply damaged, something in her had been damaged in a way that might not be able to be repaired, as if fingers and skin were touching something inside her that could not be cured.

And he thought he'd never again dare lift up his eyes.

But in the days to come his eyes often followed her in secret. The muddled memory of damp limbs, the smell that ran bitterly between narrow poorly formed thighs was turning into a source of gentleness and heat in him – she was not beautifully made, made for toil, rather misshapen: low breasts, heavy belly over narrow widely spaced legs, bone shafts clad in pimpled grey skin; but to his eyes this radiated gentleness ever more strongly, into his heart, and suddenly his heart beat hot, living beats in his chest, without shame, without fear.

And he wanted to show great gratitude. He also wanted permission to try to heal, to mend. He sometimes followed her from afar, as silent as a large dog, that was all.

But her face was helpless, pale, uncertain, it was as if she did not quite know where she was, stumbling blindly into doors and chairs – where was the man she was searching for? She behaved like a light-stunned insect, as if in a seething death-whirl.

And this had its consequences.

It wasn't exactly something that happened in the everyday. No. Day is one thing, night another. The commonplace is one thing, exception is another. And the cast or outward pull with which one is emptied of one's self. And is at once otherwise, in the exception, in the country in which great river mouths speak, they speak the oceans' tongue, forgotten, terrific.

And again time passed.

The Polish woman walked around, in search of the dead man. And her thoughts churned: a child. A child. She thought about the probe and thought that something inside might be ruined, it won't take. But then she thought that in fact it will, with a little patience it will, in a while something will happen.

And it also happened that one day Albert saw the Polish woman, gray, stooped and with that slightly muddled gaze as usual, slink around the corner and vomit among the nettles. He took in the sight of her vomiting. Among the nettles. He told himself that this must mean something. He felt heavily and at remove from reality that this sight had meaning. But he couldn't quite determine which, it felt so meaningful, to be sure he told himself with his real tongue and his real thoughts (but the real tongue and thoughts were unreal, distant) that a woman vomits when she is with child, certain actions can also lead to a woman being with child – but the sight of her and the fact of her vomiting in the nettles felt much more meaningful than this alone, it was laden with curious secret real implications, he felt that he was starting on his way, off and out, now a great many a thing could begin to happen.

What happened however was that the Polish woman's belly slowly began to grow. Time passed quickly, and slowly. The days were both heavy hot smooth to the touch, and utterly unreal. But one day Judit noticed that there was something remarkable about the Polish woman's belly. And as she studied it with her sharp gaze, it began to move under the woman's apron as if it had a life all its own. She didn't even need to look at her brother to understand how this fit together – besides he was avoiding her gaze in the most unmistakable way.

But a few days later he spoke. And his speech filled her with wonder. And thereafter with rage. And thereafter with a curious anguish – as if the real had finally ceased to exist.

For now Albert wished to marry. Albert, forty-seven years old and on this sensitive point the most ridiculed man in these parts, he now wanted to marry. To an idea such as this the Queen could only say: no. And no again. But to her dismay Albert was unshakable. He would marry. And he held fast. All the same they fought throughout the spring, it is of course no small matter for one obedient by nature to absent himself from his obedience, an obedience that ensnares him and wants to trap him from every direction. But one day in June Albert Lindgren in Bäck came driving from the farm to the Ljungby parsonage, out of the cart he helped a woman who was rather petite and odd-looking, this was the Polish woman, his brother's widow, and she was by all appearances expecting, in her sixth or seventh month, being as small as she was moving around with that large belly was not easy, she walked heavily, arduously rocking. This couple so entered the pastor's office in order to ask to have the banns published, none needed to ask the reason for this, the place was full of people and they had a most difficult time holding back their laughter, even the minister struggled to keep a straight face. The bride-to-be stood there utterly absent, above all she seemed weak in faith. There was also the difficulty that she was of a strange faith, rightfully she should be married by the Galician's priest in Bromölla but she did not insist, Albert relayed – she hadn't responded to the query; she didn't seem to understand the language at all – and he didn't want to be married by a Catholic, the Polish-priest. If now he was to be married once in his lifetime. And he looked proudly around, the minister told him dryly that putting a woman in this situation was nothing to be proud of, on the contrary, it was a rather mean feat. But Albert would not be discouraged. And on the first reading of the banns he came to the church, where he sat looking satisfied and proud and allowed himself to be regarded. And now there was talk around these parts about how Albert the virgin had at last succeeded in making one of the female sex with child, his own brother's own widow no less. And the talk was not unkind, each and everyone could see how glad and proud and happy he was, in fact no one had ever had anything against Albert;

and it could be seen from miles away that now he wanted to be happy, this was the late-in-life occasion upon which happiness was accorded, God had seen to him; he would make the most of every minute now that he suddenly had a nest like everyone else, a wife and a child on the way. And so the banns were read over them, the bride was in her eighth month, and the ceremony took place, as it were, in secret in the sacristy on an ordinary weekday afternoon, as was the custom in such cases. Albert wore a suit with a carnation stuck in his buttonhole, Judit was present – she wore a strange inscrutable expression.

And Judit looked curiously upon her brother, younger by a year, he had a big white ragged face full of peace, careworn by peace. The whole day through, he followed the Polish woman with his gaze, he did not let her out of his sight, it was as if he were always touching her from a distance, cupping his hands protectively around her; somehow he seemed to clear away any heavy thing that might be picked up, each stone she might stumble over. And this did its work deep down in the Queen who was crying, it ached and burst as if tears or moans wished to break forth from deep within that muteness, the kingdom of gentleness was so near – but then she collected herself and thought: the farm. Now I must watch out. And hold tight. For she had the idea that the Polish woman hoped to persuade Albert to buy out his sister, Albert and the Polish woman stood for two-thirds of the farm after all, in reality the Queen owned the smallest share. This idea churned in her mind – albeit she told herself this was madness, it simply couldn't be, at this point the Polish woman knew perhaps ten words of their language, overall she came across as being of uncommonly meager mind. She still appeared to be fully unaware that she was a co-owner and co-heir of the farm. But she's sly, thought the Queen, she's hiding something, she knows how to conceal her intentions.

The adversary.

And she tried to warn Albert. But he simply did not want to listen to her. For the first time it happened that he turned his back on her and walked out of the kitchen, slamming the door hard behind him, his lips trembling.

And she looked at him as one who runs the adversary's errand, who blindly flings open the door to the bringer of destruction.

The Queen entered a state of arrested motion. The cracked mask stuck to her face.

(The Queen was being consumed by a dry sickness, a corrosive sickness. Her heart was stone. Fire in the stone. The Queen had allowed the murder of her youngest son, her most beloved. Thrice behind bolting horses his dead body was dragged through the dust behind hooves in the sun, blood in the sun, around Jerusalem's walls, firmament. After this the Queen knew no peace. Then heaven bestowed on her the gift of a wonderful white bird, of the female sex besides. The Queen shouted in Jerusalem deep from within the dark city, deep from within the well: My son my son, beloved, what have I done? Cast herself down upon her face: my beloved one, what have I done to you?)

But Albert awaited the child's birth as one awaits a miracle, a drink in a place of empty burning stone where every stone radiates thirst; a great sign. And one evening he encountered the Polish woman who bore his child as well as his name and ring in the garden behind the house, the grass was tall and lashing, the rough scent of wild caraway. He approached and put his hands around her, then through her dress he could feel movement beneath her belly's taut skin. Then she looked at him and in that moment it was as if she truly saw him – him and no one else, there was a kind of recognition in her gaze, so once (at some moment, perhaps only a single one) she had sensed him and seen him, him and no one else? But then a clear membrane seemed to cover her gaze, once more it was a pure dark animal gaze, nothing else, once more there was emptiness and she was seeing inside something he knew nothing about, there he encountered someone he did not know (did not want to know, someone he knew far too well), roving there: there it was empty, there aflame. But he took hold of her again and felt the caress of the child's rolling fumbling caresses against his palms.

But something curious happened to Judit: she could not be rid of the thought that the expected child was Viktor's. She told herself this was impossible of course, it was almost two years to the day that he died. But none the less it seemed to her that this was his child. Soon it would be born. And she sensed that her arms were empty, her arms had for so many years been in want of his child.

August came. And one day the Queen felt pains. It was quite curious for she could see their coming and going upon the others' faces (and through the Polish woman's apron it too was apparent that her stomach muscles were contracting with calm frightening mechanical power) but the Queen sensed them in her own body – the prising, the breaking. The sun stood white in the sky. It was a hot day. The flies buzzed into the afternoon. Then of a sudden the Polish woman had vanished.

The farm lay silent. Impossible to keep busy – like on a deathly quiet summer Sunday (but it was Thursday). The flies buzzed. It was cool in the empty barn, cool in the dairy; but when she hesitantly pushed open the door to the barn room she was struck by a stagnant musty heat, the room faced south and facing south was a plank wall, not masonry. But no one was to be found there either.

She searched and searched through the farm, in the attic, in the earth cellar. But she found her nowhere. She didn't shout, she couldn't bring herself to. It was dead silent and everywhere hot. The sweat began to pour down her face – ice cold, she sensed, wondering, at the same time a burst of pain like none she'd ever felt before flashed through her, she bit her lower lip and muffled a cry, but afterwards it was still as if she had cried – resounding, piercing. The sun was dancing white. The heat trembled, tree and sea trembled in the heat, it was as if the whole world (and the still-as-lead smooth surface of the sea) quaked with the cry that had just been expelled or not. Then she came upon her, almost stumbling over her: at the bottom of the garden in the numbing grass-scented moist white sunlight lay her body, fingers digging into grass and earth, face turned to the earth, back twitching and writhing like a wounded worm. But not a sound could be heard, not a sigh. Only the twitching and writhing body. In one way or another Judit got her on her feet. The heat was planted like a figure of lead between them. The Polish woman's hanging head with its wrenched frightened eyes was unrecognizable. Then the heat between them melted into a thread a thin and hot thread that felt alive like hot blood seeping. It was hot and alive, it did not separate, it united. Judit placed the Polish woman's arm over her shoulders, united as a single heavy body the two women stumbled up to the house, they moved inside each other, they took the same steps, in each other's, through each other. The sun danced white. The choke pear trees gave off their sweet hot resinous bitter leaf scent.

Now Albert had permission to harness up and set off for the midwife, Judit sat with the birthing woman. The midwife arrived much later, it was already dark when Albert returned with her. And late into the evening near midnight when the hot darkness was a fragrant song of praise the Polish woman let out a long bawl like a mad dog and birthed. It was a girl. The midwife cut the umbilical cord and handed the little one to Judit: she cupped her hands around the scrawny thin hot little body. The child had pale eyes set wide. They were gleaming pale in the slits of skin. Judit bathed her in the tub with the hot water she'd prepared. The newborn screamed, in her scrunched red little face those eyes gleamed – those were the eyes she had been given. No one else's. These.

Then she was dressed and swaddled. And then Albert was called in to see his daughter.

And he saw – no one could avoid seeing it – that they were these eyes. Not anyone else's. These.

But with a gesture that resembled nothing Judit had seen from him before, so oddly self-evident, mature, he took the little girl and put her to his chest, it was clear that to him she was something all her own, one unfamiliar and mysterious, a brand new human thing – that he'd already forgiven her everything, even her eyes (the pale uncertain glittering gaze). She would be called Lydia, he said. It was the Polish woman's first name. So he went out into the darkness and found a rose among the white ramblers at the corner, it he placed upon the blanket for the woman who'd given birth.

But the Polish woman didn't want to look at him, she avoided his eyes and did not smile, the whole time she was staring questioning as if scared down at the little one now beside her on her arm: her face was empty, stiff: she held her in a curious lifeless way. She suddenly discovered with whom she'd had this girl. And with whom she hadn't had this girl. And she felt that she wished to die. Only now did she wish to die in earnest. And she felt that something inside her and perhaps all of her, belonged to death, death had breathed upon her, through and through death had taken her and marked her, she was divorced from all, now she had nothing left to do among the living.

And she lay there. The Queen had made such a fine bed, fit for a prince, linen sheets on the settle in the north chamber. Now the Polish woman lay there, a woman in childbed, after all she'd given birth to a child. But at the same time it was in some curious way as if she'd forgotten she had, she couldn't find her way back to that place in the August darkness – dark, fragrant as a song of praise – in which someone cried out and a child was born, naked and glossy wet; she looked down at the little girl beside her lying in the mangling basket, but it was a strange newborn child, utterly unlike the ones she had known before (her youngest sister swaddled with blue and red ties alongside her mother in the wide bed in Poland; later they were trampled beneath the hooves of Cossack horses, the village in flames, they fled through the snow but the riders caught up with them, catching the panting little bunch of toddlers and ungainly women was child's play); she mumbled words but no word was correct, none wielded any power against the oblivion enveloping her like something gliding like water darkening into night. She was freezing cold. Her heart fell still, shrunken in the dark silent water-chill, the oblivion-sea calmly washed its obscuring empty sea waves over her, she looked at the strange child in the basket beside her, her fingers touched the child's warm hard smooth forehead. No. It was too far away. A gray scent of reseda from the garden came through the window, the curtain waved. The child sighed in her sleep. The room was enveloped by water, oblivion.

And after only a few days she had no more milk in her breast for the little one, not a drop, and was sick and feeble.

Then the Queen took over the girl, it was only natural, the little girl moved in with her in the kitchen, there she would be, there she was also fed. The mother lay in the north chamber. The Queen sat in the kitchen with little Lydia in her arms, the warm tender one in her embrace this was her child, her tender naked head lay heavy on her arm, she looked down into the girl's eyes, down into that curious shimmering pallor. Time was torn away. What threat was there, whatever danger could there be?

But the Queen decided that because the girl in every way most resembled her side of the family, above all because she had Viktor's eyes, she'd be brought up accordingly. The girl had to be protected from her mother, this mother was strange, it was as if she bore sickness with her, it was difficult to separate a mother from her child but so it must be, the farther the better, for the sake of the child.

The Queen did not let the Polish woman out of bed, she was made to lay there in the north chamber, and in the kitchen the Queen sat with her child.

The true state of affairs passed Albert by, Judit had helped him with everything and made his every decision throughout his life, it was only clear and natural to him that his big sister Judit help with his first born, especially now that her mother was ailing and he was at a loss with such things, he hadn't seen an infant up close since Viktor, the dead man, was newborn and that was forty years ago. And it was to him self-evident that a woman in childbed lay in bed. Albeit she lay. And lay. And lay. But he presumed that in this Judit knew best, and didn't she always make the best of things? And his every thought circled the child and what the best arrangements would be for the little one and her mother. Every night when he came in he first cleansed himself thoroughly, then he put on the clean shirt and the clean socks that he really should have waited to put on until the morning thereafter: thereafter – and only thereafter – he sneaked upon his clean stocking feet over to little Lydia where she lay in her basket. Sometimes he was so bold as to take one of her hands, he let her hold his index finger and she held him tight. Thereafter he picked her up and took her in his arms and carried her to the mother in the north chamber, this was a custom he had begun, he thought a small child should sleep with its mother. She placed the girl with her mother in the settle bed, to do so he found was to exercise his rights as a husband and father of a child, other marital rights would have to be deferred until further notice.

But once he looked into Judit's face as he was picking up little Lydia from the basket in the kitchen, she was white, she had an odd look in her eyes. After that he started to wonder what wasn't right – for something was not right, wasn't right at all with his marriage, this couldn't be how it was for others, was it like this for everyone?

The Polish woman lay where she lay. Only after several weeks did she one day endeavor to get up. But she didn't seem well; at the slightest exertion sweat beaded on her brow. Albert tried to come close to her, he took her hand – but she wasn't to be gotten to, there was nowhere to begin, all was closed gliding confusion, it bore no semblance of the human, it was like digging in wind: her eyes were like an animal's, an animal in distress, a cow who'd broken its forelegs in a pit perhaps and has given up its lowing, simply lying there helpless and *looking*: she pulled away and he followed after her, wherever she went he followed, he thought that he should be to hand if she needed him. It had to happen sometime that she would need him, need someone. Then he would be at hand.

She sweated and went grayish pale; she got up early and laid back down again, and Albert came in to give her the girl. He stood there looking at them both for a while, then he left. She lay there looking at the strange child. It was September now, a red cold sunset. The girl lay there looking at her with those pale strange eyes. Then the Polish woman began to cry, she'd so wanted to have a child, and instead her child had been taken away and a strange one placed beside her. Then at once the child's face opened into a long smile. But the mother was as if far away, the dusk was red and cold, a dusking freezing fever-breath was upon her – well yes, the world was opening itself and smiling. But what did this concern her. Too far away. Dusking water. This was the last she saw, it did not reach her.

After this she lay back down and so she stayed.

And the Queen now had a child, a strong and pale-eyed deep-eyed girl-child – eyes set deep like her own, as they'd been on Viktor and on the girl growing up in Torp – . The little one was strong and ravenous though remained quite thin; the Queen dressed her in layers and layers of wool cardigans and shawls, in old children's clothing and things that had lain in chests for forty years covered with naphthalene. The child looked muffled up like a little beggar but the Queen didn't notice – the more there is, the more beautiful it is, she thought, there was always something in the Queen that leaned toward "too much," she couldn't put a limit on things, it always overflowed and ended in destruction.

And the worst part was that whenever she reached for the girl it was as if a whole life were in her hands, a whole life's arduous longing. And the longing of her hands became rough, filled with violence. And in her arms the little one grew stiff and scared, turned her face away and screamed and wouldn't eat until Albert took her. His hands were large and still, he had a way with infants that no one could have foreseen.

But the Queen felt as though she were about to swoon, everything swam around her when she was made to hand over the child.

And one day she was sitting with her. And those pale deep curious eyes looked up at her. At once a sword pierced the Queen.

For these were entirely strange eyes. They resembled no one else's. It was a stranger, someone entirely unfamiliar who lay there looking at her.

And suddenly the Queen leaned forward in an altogether mad scare and spied and spied into that little face. It was a strange unfamiliar face. It was nothing like her own. It was also nothing like Viktor's. It was altogether its own. And while she was looking and looking into that strange tender face, she discovered there was an altogether unfamiliar brittle sensitivity in it, something quaking and elusively weak and fine and close to breaking, the girl in her arms was not who she'd taken her for. She'd been mistaken. And it was then at once that she sensed a sickly sweet smell – perhaps like the sweet unwashed smell of poverty – was emanating from the child, her tender heat. Which she had been holding so tight and close.

The Polish woman, she lay and lay.

Albert began in earnest to say that something was not right here, this couldn't be what marriage was like – it was now the month of October and the girl was three months old and all the while the Polish woman lay in her bed in the north chamber, her state was absolute, she made no further attempt to get up. And she'd begun to struggle to take in food. Judit carried full plates into her room. No one could say that the sick woman was being starved, no one could say anything but that she was in receipt of the best care. But the plates were left to stand, the food had been merely prodded at the edges as if nibbled by a mouse – the midday meal would stand until evening, the evening meal until the morning thereafter. But this is all the Polish woman would eat and nothing more. Thus passed October. And Albert wondered what to do, every evening he wondered ever more lost what manner of desolate wilderness he'd happened upon. But when he asked himself, this memory couldn't reach that heat, as alive as a spring. Her face and the skewed gray limbs emerged. In the same way as with Judit who was called Queen this was a question of faith, one had to believe that the living person was somewhere behind the ghost-mask, behind the face of death, the captive inside the stone was not to be abandoned.

So then it was November. And the landscape, stripped. The fields so wide. The sky low and desolate above the sea. And on one such cloudy windy damp twilight he came into the kitchen, as usual to carry little Lydia in to her mother. He arrived with the half-sleeping infant in the north chamber. Then the Polish woman was not there. He thought she might be out doing something (she did go out for such things), he sat down and as he waited regarded his daughter who was keeping one eye open and the other shut.

But a long while passed and the Polish woman did not appear.

He began to worry, carried out the child and placed her in the basket and told Judit he had to go search outside – Judit who was standing at the stove, had not seen a thing, she said, perhaps the Polish woman had snuck out through the great door. Upon closer inspection, the great door was unbolted.

Albert searched the whole farm. Barn, stall, box and loft, he also searched the attic and the earth cellar. But the Polish woman was nowhere to be found. It was windy, the smell of sea came in with the wind. He noted that it would be dark soon. And he had to find her before dark. And he prayed to God that he may find her before dark. Then at once, he didn't know how, it was crystal clear that he should take the path across the field down to the pine grove with the well, the wind-moaning grove around which the road curved. He started upon the path, he ran, finally he couldn't run fast enough, it was as if he were flying, his heart flying ahead of him on the path toward the well, it had wings. The grove's smell of wet needles. Brown grass and dead patches of nettles. And there she lay beside the well, she lay there in the brown wet grass with her arms under her head as if she were sleeping. Covering the well (which surely had not been used for fifty years) was a large flat stone she had clearly not had the strength to push aside. And now she lay there in the dead damp grass. And the smell of sea came with the wind.

He knelt beside her and slowly stroked the hair from her cheek. Then he saw that her eyes were wide-open, she was looking straight ahead but she did not see him. And then his gaze opened and he saw at once how she was transformed in an awful way, skeletal, the gray clammy loose skin plastered tight across her cheekbones, in her cheeks were great hollows, her eyes shining like water mirroring the sky. And with this he understood that something was wrong, broken, there was nothing to do about it; this marriage of his was altogether peculiar, something unto itself, nothing about it resembled that of others – but it was his here and now. And the woman who lay there in the wet dead grass, was she, no one else, she who was his, and he had her, and this was his life, such was his life, this was how it would be. He lifted her up, she was light as a bird, no more than a small pile of slender bones and the skin that held them together, he carried her up the path to the farm, his broken bird.

The Queen walked there mighty, dead. She stood in the twilight, shrieking: My crown, my crown! Calling out across the sea. A crown of blood she bore tightly below the dome of her skull. But inside her Judit was crying, she was not old, she wanted to slip out of the Queen's stiff dead garb, she didn't want to bear the Queen's injurious jewels –

– Judit wanted to take the sick woman's confused hand, together they would seek the beloved one, he who healed, but the sick woman was so fuddled and foul, so unrecognizable and warped and wrecked, she did probably understand her father's approach to such things, but this warped and stinking being wasn't one she could take in hand, it simply couldn't be that this was her unborn sister, the one miscarried decomposed –

– and inside the Queen, Judit was crying out in a frightful anguish, wild fear: She is me! She is me!

And it was as if the same bodies, limbs soldered together, mouths and lips birthed the same cry: it was inside her like a shape, a body, a strange beast with two backs.

Then came the village doctor and said his piece on the matter. And the taxi cab was summoned. And Albert took the Polish woman, who was dressed like a doll and sat on a kitchen chair, waiting without realizing she was waiting, and he led her to little Lydia's basket so they could say goodbye to each other, the little girl was awake and lay looking up and was probably also looking at the silent woman who stood there – but the Polish woman did not look at her, she but stood there – clothes hanging off her like off a clothes hanger. The taxi cab arrived; and Albert took her to the receiving ward in Kristianstad, from where she would later go on to St. Lars in Lund, there she would stay, she lay in a bed and did not move, this did not change, she thought she lay at the bottom of a well with slippery walls deep down in empty water darkness, fingers gaining no purchase, they were scraped bloody on the slippery stones, this did not change, years and time passed over the woman who lay in her bed at the bottom of a well, her bloody skinned-raw chewed fingers scraped on stones, every now and then a feeble gurgling groan might escape her.

But after Albert accompanied his spouse to the receiving ward and returned in the evening (he arrived with the last train), he came into the kitchen, he took a seat across from his sister and looked at her. He didn't say a word. Just looked and looked.

It was dark now. It was windy out. But the child kept breathing in her basket over in the corner.

After a while the Queen began to cry.

And the Queen cried.

The Queen wailed and shouted over the walls, a wild lamenting cry broke forth and broke down, stones burst, walls collapsed, the tears came ever closer, for years and decades the walls, the eroding rocks, the dead rock slabs had been breathing only thirst and fire.

Now the tears came ever closer, it was a wild disintegrating cry, tears fell from the stones.

Then the Queen sensed that Albert was coming to her. She stared up in perfect silence, she stared at him as if seeing him for the first time, then she flung herself into his arms and hid her face on his shoulder. Albert then slowly placed his cheek upon his sister's head. They stood close together, holding each other. There they stood. Through the window the sea appeared as a shadow in the darkness. The surf could be seen in the dark. From the great inosculated pair of humans could be heard a deep long sigh as when a horse sighs. Then Albert placed his hands around his sister's head so that he hid her from herself.

Then the Queen went off and picked up the strange obscure child from the basket and held her on her arm. And the Queen cried. But this time the little one offered no resistance: and the Queen saw that the child's face was sheer weakness and sensitivity in motion, in those pale uncertain deep eyes was a curious shadow of vulnerability, gentleness, she resembled no one else, she was brand new, come from far far away.

Thus passed the time. It was beyond all time. Albert made a long journey, all the way to Lund; when he returned he was silent, he said nothing of how it had been. By Christmas little Lydia could sit up in her basket, there she sat, looking out over her world, and rattled a rattle filled with goose feathers, it was all they'd been able to give her for Christmas, money was very tight that year. The Queen sometimes said to her brother: Now it's taking a turn for the worse. It's truly taking a turn. But he encouraged her, saying how could anything harm them now that the little one existed, doesn't the Lord provide for even the smallest sparrow to feed its children. And also to the Queen it seemed in the end that little Lydia was a bastion. And when all was said and done everything did come together for them that year as well, hadn't they just made it through Christmas and New Year and a good way into the new year, and little Lydia was sitting up and laughing and rattling her goose rattle.

In January came the snow. Then followed a long period, several weeks, of intense cold and invariably beautiful weather. The sea froze over, the villages lay so dark, seemed so cramped and dim in contrast to the vast blinding white expanses all around. Through the low windows the blinding ice-light burst in.

It was the deepest cold. At night Landö lighthouse swept its light through the dark, across the snow fields where farms, trees, nighttime wanderers were caught like insects in the beam – then the darkness again, soundless the light flies across the ice, at the very edge of the ice the clear mute black water keeps watch, in perfect silence.

At the end of January, in the middle of the deepest cold, the Queen finally took on a task that she had long been drawn toward, she told herself it was a good thing too – but above all she felt a sort of pull and a suction, it came from deep below, deep down at the soul's bottom it resided, it grew ever stronger, every more curious. And so she traveled to Lund.

There she sat beside the bed, she sat there for as long as the visiting hours lasted, she tried placing a row of sweets on the sheet before the infirm one but the woman in the bed never once reacted.

This became the Queen's habit. Each month she traveled there (Albert seldom, he couldn't bring himself to). Each month the Queen in Bäck arrived and sat there by the bed, looking. Time and years passed over them, over the woman who arrived to sit by the bed, and over the outstretched unmoving body in the bed. Her eyes shone ever emptier, every larger in their hollows. With time they sank in. Through the red blanket was the outline of the body with its slender chest, the sunken bowl of the pelvis, the shafts of thigh bone. The neck twisted back was skin and sinew. The Queen sat and looked. So went life.

The Queen in Bäck became peculiar with the years, she seemed to turn inward on herself, her connection to the world around became ever more halting, it became such that she could only with the utmost exertion manage to come into contact with her surroundings – and she acquired a helplessly confused expression of pride: if it doesn't work then it doesn't work, it's not worth the trouble. But Albert and little Lydia (who grew up to have dark hair, dark braids down to her waist, but a quite rugged colorless face) cared for her with great attentiveness, they were two cautious shy beings very alike in temperament and sensitivity. Finally the Queen stopped going into the village: in the summer she tended to her lilies and the other flowers, never had the garden been so beautiful, it was like a paradise (and enclosed like paradise, no outsider was granted entry anymore, the postman had to stop at the front gate; but all had heard tell of the loveliness and sweet perfume of the Queen's garden) – in winter she thought of seeds and bulbs. Her hair had gone pure white. And now it fell to Albert to handle everything, it was what it was but it was better than one might have expected – heaven helps the innocent, it was said in these parts. The girl was of great help to him, she accompanied him always and loved her father very much, she fell silent in the company of others, she was withdrawn and had a timid disposition, the expression in her rugged grayish face was shy and friendly. Accordingly, Albert seemed to find his way in this, for him, utterly impossible life where he was forced to act and make decisions and go to the store and even to the bank so as to be granted respite from payments, all this he managed – not like the Queen, but nonetheless serviceably; he seemed to stand ever taller and in time it became almost impossible to imagine that he hadn't always been a frank warm-hearted man who was easy to speak with, easy to borrow from however little he himself had. As for the Queen, one rarely saw more than a flash of her snow-white crown of hair behind the curtains in the window of the north chamber, mostly she sat in there, its fire was lit nowadays – even in the summer sometimes, she'd begun to feel very cold. But once a month Albert drove her to the station, then she made her trip, however little money was in the house it would stretch to the Queen's trip to Lund. But in the winter of 1940 she developed a kidney ailment, had several stays at the hospital, finally she was sent home – thus she took to the bed in the chamber and faded away. After this, she did not have the energy to travel down to Lund and see the Polish woman in the bed, it contributed to her fading, she spoke constantly of the woman there outstretched – as if they were two trees of the same root, to not be able to see her there in bed was as if to be severed from her root, from her mother-tree in the earth. Young Lydia sat with her. The Queen often wanted to hold her hand and she wanted constant reassurance that the girl forgave her, then she entered into confusion, mixing the girl up with her mother. Young Lydia caressed her hand. Thus passed the days and so died the Queen like the lilies bend and wither: still, white, yellowing.

AFTERWORD

It was the Swedish writer Mirja Unge who first talked to me about Birgitta Trotzig. This was in the winter of 2000, I'd just turned thirty, Mirja is four years younger. I went to Stockholm to interview her for a literary magazine, and she told me she was reading Birgitta Trotzig. No one had ever mentioned Trotzig to me before. I was so taken with Mirja Unge's work – she has her own very free and physical way of being in her writing, in the tone and rhythm, as if the words are earth in her hands –and I wanted to read Trotzig to see what was behind Mirja, as if there was a forest there, and in that forest somewhere was Birgitta Trotzig. The first thing I read by Trotzig was *The Marsh King's Daughter*. I carried on from there. It felt like coming home down into the depths of the underworld, where what truly is essential and real in our lives – the dark, vulnerable, raw and exposed – is what the books are about. The "plot" of a novel is almost absent in Trotzig's work, she is deep inside us, where we yearn and blindly grope, and are helpless and small. Where we hurt others and can find no way back. She inhabits the mythic space within us, the divine, where we all, no matter how wretched we are, nevertheless are still made of light.

When I first began reading Birgitta Trotzig I was at a point in my life when I'd manoeuvred myself all the way out into the edgelands of the living, of life, away from other people. I'd broken off with my mother. I'd left my publishers because I didn't trust the new editorial director they'd installed, I didn't want my books handled by him. Those publishers had been my family throughout the whole of my adult life, I belonged there. But then all of a sudden I couldn't be there anymore, not without the risk of my books, all that I was, being pressed into a narrative that wasn't mine. So I put out a novel with a different publisher, but it was like being homeless, destitute. I didn't know what to do. I'd walked away from everyone, it was my own doing, and I knew that no one was going to come and bring me back. So I was out there, in the edgelands, I walked endlessly in snow and ice on the narrow roads of Nesodden, and it was as if I wasn't hooked up to the world anymore, walking there while listening to Radioteatret's version of Ibsen's *Brand* over and over again. That was what I did. And I read Martin Heidegger's *The Origin of the Work of Art*, I read the Norwegian philosopher Jon Wetlesen's long introduction to a work by Meister Eckhart, a German mystic of the thirteenth century. Quietly, over and over, this was what I did. And then I read Birgitta Trotzig. I didn't know what to do, all I knew was that I needed to find a way into the warmth again, to where others were. Either I could find a way to belong, or – well, what?

A notion of Heidegger's beamed into me, that truth happens, as conflict, in the work of art. In Wetlesen's introduction it was the circle, the way Eckhart meets contradiction, opposition, conflict, by drawing a circle that embraces both sides. I'm not sure if that's exactly the way he puts it, but it was what stayed with me, the notion of 'drawing a bigger circle,' the realization that this was what I had to reach out toward, within myself.

Birgitta Trotzig was the one who showed me how language can open itself out and embrace. I needed to soften up, I needed a softer language, and it was she who showed me it was possible. On the first page of *The Marsh King's Daughter* a woman comes walking barefoot across a field by the open sea one summer morning, the simple line of her walking while circular medusa-like movements expand the moment: "All steamed with wetness, pearling and rejoicing. She walked through the buzzing fragrant singing summer morning ... Through the streaming blinding sea-surging light she walked." By placing the adjectives up against each other like this, Trotzig conjurs a soft, gliding movement the reader feels in her body, with each adjective the image opens out and expands further. Language is both meaning and music, image and body. Something is *held* by this language. You can *lean* into it, as if the language itself were mother, as if the language itself were hands. To me it was trust, it seemed there was in Trotzig's writing a trust of *being* itself, which I simply allowed to percolate in me, I read nearly everything she wrote, I doused myself in her language, which dared to lean, which holds, which gives. And this made it possible for me to write *The Pastor*, for me a musical novel in which it's the language's very capacity to *hold* us that comprises the novel's hope, a novel I wrote so that what happens inside the pastor, Liv (whose name, in a novel that exists on the edges of death, means *life*), might also happen inside me, that she return to the fold, to the community of others, the living, regardless of strife and conflict, I leaned profoundly in its writing towards rhythm and tone, which is where that novel expresses its true purpose.

To me, Trotzig is the one who says: trust the language, it holds, it withstands, lean into it, let yourself be held.

Queen is a novel I've read many times, I think because it depicts a character whose predicament is so close to my own: being strong and having to endure, making oneself hard and shutting onself off to others, because you know no other way of coping. That longing for love. Every time I read it, I'm moved by the unfathomableness of Viktor and the Polish woman, who in the chaotic teeming crowd in New York suddenly just hold onto each other, as if the world were a bottomless void through which they are falling, and all they can do is cling to this random other beside them. And thus they come together.

I've long sensed in myself that I'm drawn back to Trotzig's work whenever I'm feeling low, as if there's something in her writing that's made to accompany the depressive state. I've needed her writing as a place to go with all that feels heavy, for Trotzig does not look away but is able to look deeply into the pain of being shut out, from others, from the sky and the self. But reading *Queen* once again now, the ending opened itself out to me in a new way and the novel felt much lighter than I've felt it before. This makes me think that now finally I might be ready to also take in the grace contained in Birgitta Trotzig's gaze. The ending reminds me of Ibsen's *Brand*, where the eponymous hard-nosed pastor eventually realizes what he has done and weeps, softens, and opens up, which also happens with Judit. But Trotzig's novel is in a sense both deeper and more elevated: "and inside the Queen, Judit was crying out in a frightful anguish, wild fear: She is me! She is me!" Judit sees the other, who she has forsaken and cast out, sees that she is not Other, but Same. She is me. And every month, Judit goes and sits by the other's sickbed. The way Judit needs to be close to this other broken one, and the way Judit longs for forgiveness. And that perhaps it is the same thing.

HANNE ØRSTAVIK
translated by Martin Aitken